Four Weddings and a Funeral

RICHARD CURTIS

Level 5

Retold by Cherry Gilchrist
Series Editors: Andy Hopkins and Jocelyn Potter

Pearson Education Limited
Edinburgh Gate, Harlow,
Essex CM20 2JE, England
and Associated Companies throughout the world.

ISBN: 978-1-4058-8244-6

First published by Transworld Publishers Ltd 1994
Penguin Books edition first published 1999
This edition first published 2008

ARP impression 98

Original copyright © Polygram Film Produktion GMbH 1993
Text copyright © Penguin Books 1999
All rights reserved

The moral right of the adapter has been asserted

Adaptation of this screenplay by kind permission of Richard Curtis

The right of Richard Curtis to be identified as the original author of this
work has been asserted in accordance with sections 77 and 78 of the
Copyright Designs and Patents Act

Typeset by Graphicraft Ltd, Hong Kong
Set in 11/14pt Bembo
Printed and bound in Great Britain by Ashford Colour Press Ltd
SWTC/09

Acknowledgements
The publisher would like to thank the following for
their kind permission to reproduce their photographs:
Cover images: *Front and back:* **The Kobal Collection:** Polygram / Channel 4 / Working Title; **CD
Cover:** *Onbody:* **The Kobal Collection:** Polygram / Channel 4 / Working Title

Gratefully acknowledges that Rowan Atkinson, Simon Callow,
Charlotte Coleman, Hugh Grant, David Haig, John Hannah, Andie MacDowell,
Kristin Scott Thomas and Sophie Thompson have given permission for
photographs from *Four Weddings and a Funeral* to be used in return for a
donation of £1,000 for The Diana, Princess of Wales Memorial Fund,
registered charity number: 1064238
Published by Pearson Education Ltd

*Every effort has been made to trace the copyright holders and we apologise in advance for any unintentional omissions.
We would be pleased to insert the appropriate acknowledgement in any subsequent edition of this publication.*

For a complete list of the titles available in the Pearson English Readers series, visit
www.pearsonenglishreaders.com.
Alternatively, write to your local Pearson Education office or to Pearson English Readers
Marketing Department, Pearson Education, Edinburgh Gate, Harlow, Essex CM20 2JE, England.

Contents

Introduction

'How are you doing, Charles?'
'Actually, not great.' says Charles. 'Not great at all, really. Why am
I always at weddings but never getting married? What does it mean?
Maybe it's me – I'm the problem.'
'Oh, rubbish!' says Matthew.

It's summer and it's Saturday morning, and Charles is still asleep.
He should be on his way to his friends' wedding – his friend has
asked him to be the 'best man'! But Charles is always late, and
he is always going to weddings. 'Why am I always at weddings,
but never my own?' he asks. He has had plenty of girlfriends, but
he has never met the right woman. He is worried that he never
will. One of his old girlfriends, Henrietta, thinks that he has a big
problem with women. But then he meets the beautiful Carrie,
and he thinks she is the right woman. She likes him too. The
trouble is, he can't decide quickly enough, and he doesn't tell her
how he feels. She marries another man.

This is a romantic and very funny story about love. It takes us
to four weddings. Three of the weddings are for Charles's friends.
There are a few surprises at the fourth one. It is also a story
about friendship. In Charles's group of friends we meet the lively
Scarlett, Tom and Fiona, the rich brother and sister, and Gareth,
the 'rude, fat man'.

There is sadness too. One of the group dies suddenly. The
funeral is an important moment in the story, when Charles finally
tries to sort out his life . . . but does he succeed?

The film *Four Weddings and a Funeral* was first shown in cinemas
in 1994. English actor Hugh Grant plays the 'hero' Charles, and
American model Andie MacDowell is Carrie. Other famous

actors in the film include Kristin Scott Thomas as Fiona and Rowan Atkinson (who is better known as Mr Bean) as the nervous priest. Richard Curtis wrote the story. Curtis and Grant worked together again on another British film, *Notting Hill* (1999), this time with Julia Roberts as the romantic lead.

Four Weddings and a Funeral was directed by Mike Newell, whose other films include *Harry Potter and the Goblet of Fire* (2005) and *Donnie Brasco* (1997).

Richard Curtis came up with the idea for the film when he was looking through some old diaries. He realised he'd been to more than sixty weddings in the previous eleven years. Writing the story took a while, as he had to rewrite some lines as many as seventeen times! Curtis's girlfriend Emma was his closest critic. If she didn't like a page of his film story, she wrote the letters CDB on the page. 'CDB' meant 'Could Do Better'.

It took a long time to choose a title for this film. More than fifty suggestions were made, including *Always Late* and *In Love in England*. The final title was a good choice. Original music was written for the film, but it included *Love is All Around* by Wet Wet Wet.

The four weddings and the funeral take place all over the UK, including one in a Scottish castle. There wasn't much money available to make this film, however, and it was actually all filmed in the south-east of England. The 'Scottish' castle is in Sussex and the film extras at the weddings had to bring their own dresses and suits.

The story is told in the present tense in this book; you feel as if you are watching the film as you read. Each scene is described as it happens.

Who's who in this story

Charles is attractive and unmarried; he's had many girlfriends but he can't find the right woman.

Carrie is a beautiful American woman who's had many boyfriends.

Scarlett shares a flat with Charles; she's not his girlfriend and she's looking for the right man.

Fiona is clever and elegant, unlike her brother. She hasn't got a boyfriend; she's in love with someone who doesn't love her.

Tom is Fiona's brother; he's a rich but not very clever friend of Charles; no girlfriend, but he's looking for love.

Henrietta is an old girlfriend of Charles and still wants to marry him; people call her 'Duck Face' behind her back.

Gareth is a loud and lively friend of Charles; he enjoys his food and drink and lives with his boyfriend Matthew.

Matthew is quieter than Gareth, and kind and intelligent. He and Gareth have been together a long time.

John is Henrietta's brother; he's very boring.

David is Charles's younger brother; he's deaf, and he and Charles communicate by sign language.

Serena is an affectionate young woman; she learns sign language so she can talk to David

Bernard is Tom's best friend. He likes Lydia.

Lydia is Laura's bridesmaid at the first wedding. She's not interested in Bernard at first.

Who's who in this story

Chapter 1　The First Wedding

You are invited to the wedding of Angus and Laura
on May 1st at St John's Church, Stoke Clandon, Somerset

It's Angus and Laura's wedding day, and Charles is going to be their best man. The best man has to look after the bridegroom and give him the wedding ring. The best man also has to be at the church on time, but Charles is never punctual. He is not even awake yet. The alarm clock rings loudly next to his bed. He reaches out his hand, turns it off, and goes back to sleep.

The wedding is in the west of England, which is at least two or three hours by car from London, where Charles lives. Some of his other friends are awake though. They'll be at the wedding before Charles. In their large, fine house, Tom and Fiona are up and getting ready to go. They are brother and sister, and they come from a very rich family. They are opposite types of people: Fiona is a tall, elegant and clever woman; Tom is a happy, but not very intelligent, man.

Tom enjoys his food, and he's now eating a large breakfast while Fiona chooses what to wear. Finally, she zips herself into a smart dress. She goes downstairs to the dining-room and the maid gives her a cup of black coffee. She quickly drinks it, and they set off. It's Saturday, so the traffic is not too bad, but they mustn't delay any longer.

On their way out of London, they call for Gareth and Matthew, who live together in an attractive, country-style house. Matthew is a cool but kind, sympathetic person – a Scotsman in his thirties. Gareth is a large, fat man of about forty-five. His hair is a little grey, but his beard is still black. He likes to wear quite elegant, but very bright clothes. He loves to joke, and is often quite rude to other people. Gareth and Matthew are boyfriends.

'Late! You're late!' he shouts, pointing at his watch. But Tom and Fiona know Gareth well, and don't take any notice.

They are not as late as Charles though, who is still asleep. Finally, the sun shines on to him through the bedroom curtains and he wakes up. He takes the alarm clock off the table near his bed and looks at it.

'Oh God!' he says. He is really awake this time.

Charles is thirty-three years old, good-looking, and always late. He jumps out of bed and rushes in to Scarlett's bedroom. Charles and Scarlett share a flat together. They are friends, but not lovers. Her room is a terrible mess – there are clothes everywhere. He picks up her red alarm clock and puts it under her nose. She opens her eyes sleepily.

'Oh hell!'

Scarlett is twenty-five, lively, and a real London girl. You can hear it in her voice – she's certainly not from an upper-class family!

They hurry to get ready, and run out to the car, carrying some of their formal wedding clothes with them. The car is Charles's, and it's very old. The engine won't start.

'Oh God! Oh hell!' says Charles. 'Right, we'd better take yours.'

'Mine?' says Scarlett. 'But it only goes at forty miles an hour!'

Charles drives her car so fast along the motorway that it shakes. It is a very small, red car, and it's also very old and rusty. The engine makes a terrible noise. Scarlett can't have looked after it very well!

'What road are we looking for?' asks Charles.

Scarlett has a map, but she hasn't looked at it yet. She picks it up just as they pass a motorway exit sign.

'I hope it's not the B359,' Charles says when he sees the sign behind him.

Scarlett finds the right place on the map. 'It's the B359,' she says proudly.

'Damn!' says Charles. He suddenly puts his foot on the brake and starts to drive backwards along the motorway. There is a lorry coming up fast behind them, and there is nearly a terrible accident. Charles turns the car on to the exit road.

'Oh, hell and damn!' he says again.

♦

It is a beautiful sunny day not long after noon as they arrive at the small church in the peaceful countryside. The church bells are ringing and all the other guests are already inside. Charles and Scarlett jump out of the car. Charles hasn't finished dressing and neither has Scarlett. They quickly put on the rest of their wedding clothes. For Charles, it's a formal suit. But Scarlett is wearing a bright orange dress with purple around the waist, and an orange hat to match. Charles tries to help her do it up at the back, but the zip gets stuck.

'Hell, hellish hell!' says Charles, pulling at the zip.

'Damn and hell!' says Scarlett. She tries to get his tie straight. A very large smart car drives up behind them. The bride is coming.

She gets out of the car in her beautiful white wedding dress. One of her bridesmaids helps her. They are both holding wonderful bunches of flowers.

'Oh no!' Charles says, and they begin to run towards the church. They smile and wave at the bride as they pass her.

The church is full of flowers and all the women guests are wearing elegant hats. Charles and Scarlett look around and finally see their friends, Fiona and Tom, Gareth and Matthew. They go over to them.

Fiona says to Charles, 'There is a sort of greatness in your lateness.'

'Thanks,' Charles replies. 'I have to work hard at it, you know.'

Scarlett sits down with them, but Charles puts a pink flower in the buttonhole of his jacket and walks on up the church to Angus, the bridegroom, who is waiting nervously for his best man.

'Sorry, sorry,' says Charles. 'There's no excuse, I know. I'll kill myself afterwards, if you like.'

'It doesn't matter,' says Angus. 'If you hadn't come Tom would have taken your place.'

'Thanks, Tom – you're wonderful! What a terrible haircut though!' Charles jokes.

'You haven't forgotten the ring, have you?' asks Angus. The best man is always given the ring to bring to the church.

'No, no, of course not.' Charles touches his pocket confidently. But he is secretly alarmed. Where is the ring? When Angus isn't looking, he searches for it in his pockets, but they are all empty. Oh God! He must have left it at home!

Just then, an attractive girl in a large black hat and white jacket walks into the church.

Charles and several other guests turn to look at her.

'Late!' says Charles. 'I hate it when people are late! *Hate* it.'

This makes Angus smile a little and he seems less nervous now. Then the wedding music starts.

'Here we go!' says Charles, and Angus turns round to look at his bride, who is walking up the aisle towards him. Laura is holding on to her father's arm, and she's wearing a very expensive white wedding dress. She has two little bridesmaids, and one older bridesmaid, a young woman called Lydia.

'Oh, isn't she beautiful!' breathes Scarlett.

'You're blind,' says Fiona sharply. 'She looks like a big white cake.'

'Dear friends, I am so happy to welcome you here today,' the priest begins the service. 'Welcome to our church on this wonderful day for Angus and Laura!'

But Charles is looking around him, wondering what to do

4

about the ring. When he sees the girl in the black hat, he starts to think about other things – she's very attractive. Then he remembers that there is a more urgent problem. Everyone is singing now. He tries to make one of his friends notice him, but has no luck.

At last Matthew looks at him. Charles points at his own ring finger and the pain on his face tells Matthew what the problem is.

'Please! Help me!' Charles silently makes the words with his lips.

Matthew whispers to Gareth, but Gareth holds out both hands to show that there is no ring on them. He whispers to Fiona, and to several more friends too. None of them is wearing a ring. Charles will be in big trouble! The singing is coming to an end now.

Scarlett is singing very loudly and enthusiastically but not very well. Matthew interrupts her.

'Scarlett!' whispers Matthew. She is their last hope. She smiles back at him innocently. When the priest begins to read the next words of the service, Matthew nods to Charles – yes, they've got something!

'I'll be back in a moment!' Charles says to the groom, who looks alarmed.

The priest continues to speak: 'Do you promise to love her...?' while Charles goes down the side of the church to find Matthew.

Angus, the bridegroom, is saying 'I do.'

Matthew hands something to Charles, and Charles looks surprised at what Matthew has given him.

'It's the best I could do,' whispers Matthew.

Charles rushes back to the front of the church.

'Do you have the ring?' asks the priest.

When he sees it, he is quite surprised too. Angus puts the ring on to his bride's finger. It is in the shape of a large, brightly-coloured plastic heart.

While the happy couple are signing their names at the back of the church, the bride's sister and her boyfriend come forwards with a guitar to sing pop music. It's an old Barry Manilow song.

Gareth holds his head in his hands. Then he pretends to shoot himself. He is letting everybody know that it is one of the most terrible things he has ever heard.

At last it's time to leave the church. When the bride, the groom and the guests walk out of the church they look very happy. Everybody is smiling and chatting. Charles catches up with the girl in the black hat outside.

'That's a great hat,' he says.

'Thanks – I bought it specially,' she smiles at him. He can hear from her accent that she's American.

Now it's time for the wedding photos. The photographer arranges the bride, the groom and the family in groups for the different pictures. A little boy spoils one of them when he tries to hide under the big skirts of the bride's wedding dress. He thinks it's funny – but the others don't.

Charles and his friends all get together in their own group to chat. There's Matthew and Gareth, there's Fiona and Tom, and of course the lively Scarlett. There's Charles's brother, David, too, who is deaf and communicates in sign language using his hands. And there's also Bernard, who is Tom's best friend – he is like Tom, a kind man, but not very clever.

Tom enjoyed the wedding and so did Bernard.

'I thought it was good, very good,' says Tom. 'What did you think?'

'Oh yes, good, very good,' replies Bernard.

'Scarlett,' says Gareth, 'what an amusing dress! Purple for the Christian church, and orange for the wild natural world. Just like the meaning of the wedding itself, don't you think?'

'Yes – that's right,' says Scarlett, who doesn't really know what he means.

'Does anybody know,' asks Charles, 'who the girl in the black hat is?'

They all look at her. She is standing not far away, talking to somebody's grandmother.

'Her name's Carrie,' says Fiona.

'She's pretty,' says Charles.

'Awful girl!' says Fiona. 'She's American. She used to work at *Vogue*, the fashion magazine.* She lives in America now, and she only goes out with very smart, elegant people. So you can forget about her, Charles.'

Fiona is not completely serious.

'It's a good thing you told me,' says Charles, who knows this. 'Thanks.'

The bride and groom leave the guests and get into their car. They look very happy. People wave at them as the car is being driven away.

'Right,' says Gareth. 'It's time for the reception.'

♦

The guests have to walk through a farm to get to the reception. It is very pretty, but Tom steps in some cow mess.

'Did any of you do this too?' he asks, looking at his shoe.

'Typical!' says Fiona. 'Only my brother could do that!'

'Well,' said Tom, 'I might find love at the reception. There might be a really nice girl there! I don't want to spoil my good luck with a horrible smell!'

He stops to clean his shoe, and the others walk on towards the house. The bride and groom and their families are standing outside in a line. Everybody has to shake their hands and congratulate them as they go past.

'I never know what to say,' says Fiona.

* A magazine which is very famous in Britain and America.

7

'It's easy. Just say, "You must be very proud,"' Matthew advises her. 'That's what everyone says.'

'God, no!' says Fiona.

They walk up the line.

'You must be very proud of your daughter,' says Fiona, as she shakes the hand of the bride's father.

The reception is being held in a very large and smart tent, on the grass at the front of the house. It is full of flowers, and looks very beautiful. The guests are elegant too, but in a comfortable, not too rich way. Most of the men are wearing dark suits, and a lot of the women have dresses with flowers on them. The drinks are being served by waiters and waitresses, and at the back of the tent, the band is getting ready to play.

Charles pushes through the crowd, trying to find Carrie. But when he finally sees her, she is already talking to a good-looking man.

'The rat!' says Charles. He goes back to the drinks table and takes two glasses of wine. When he turns round again, she is alone. He offers her a drink.

'Oh – hello!' he says brightly. 'Do you want one of these?'

'Thank you,' Carrie replies.

Charles badly wants to talk to her, but he can't think of anything to say.

'Ah – mmm –'

The situation is rather embarrassing for them both.

Before he can think of something, another man joins them. This is John, who is about thirty-eight, but behaves like a man of sixty. He is very formal.

'Hello Charles,' he says.

'Ah, hello, dear John – how are you? This is . . .'

'Carrie,' answers Carrie for him.

'I'm delighted to meet you. My name's John.'

They are all silent for a moment – who is going to speak

first? Charles decides to be the first.

'So, John, how's that lovely girlfriend of yours?'

'She's not my girlfriend now,' he replies stiffly.

'Oh dear – well, don't be sad! I heard that she was still seeing old Toby de Lisle! She needed two men, you know!'

'She is now my wife,' says John, even more stiffly.

The situation is now even more embarrassing than before.

'Excellent, excellent!' says Charles, very uncomfortably. 'May I congratulate you? And is there the sound of little feet yet? You know – babies, and all that? No? Oh well, plenty of time for that, isn't there?'

'Excuse me,' says Carrie, amused. She walks away.

Charles tells himself that he is a fool. If he hadn't said those stupid things, Carrie wouldn't have gone, and John wouldn't have been hurt. He hits his head against a tree on purpose, then tries to say hello to an old lady who is walking past. She thinks he is crazy.

Fiona has found a man called Gerald to talk to. He looks innocent, but a bit strange too. He is wearing a dark suit and a black pullover.

'What do you do?' she asks him.

'I'm studying to be a priest,' he answers.

'Good God,' says Fiona. 'Do you do weddings?'

'Not yet – I will do later, of course. It'll make me very nervous, I can tell you!' He laughs uncomfortably.

'That's just like the first time one has sex, isn't it?' Fiona says sweetly.

Gerald is even more embarrassed now. 'Ah – well, I suppose so –'

'Not so much mess, though,' Fiona continues, but Gerald can't reply at all now.

David has come over to talk to Charles, his brother. Charles knows sign language for the deaf very well, and has communicated like this with David since they were children.

'How are you doing?' David asks with his hands.

'Do you remember that time when we were playing with the engine on Dad's motor boat, and my leg was almost cut off?'

'Yes.'

'Well, this is worse.'

Somebody has been watching David – a pretty girl with long red hair. She is wearing a bright yellow hat. Her name is Serena. She points at David.

'Who's that boy over there in the grey suit?' she asks Matthew.

'His name's David,' Matthew answers.

'He's very attractive, isn't he?' she says.

'Yes – I've always thought so.'

'Why are they using their hands like that?' she asks.

'He can't hear. He's deaf,' says Matthew.

'Oh – good heavens!'

'Silent, but very attractive,' Matthew continues.

And now the father of the bride tells everyone that dinner is being served. He asks them to go into the tent and sit down. They all find their way to their tables. John sits down next to his wife, not as happy with her as he was earlier now that he knows about Toby de Lisle. Carrie sits next to George, another stiff and boring type of man who read a piece from the Bible very loudly at the wedding service. Scarlett sits down next to a complete stranger, and gives him a big kiss on the mouth.

'Hi – my name's Scarlett! Don't let me drink too much – I get much too friendly!'

Charles, as best man, has to sit on the top table with the family. He sits down next to an old man, who looks annoyed.

'How do you do – my name is Charles.'

'Don't be stupid!' the old man says angrily. 'Charles died twenty years ago!'

'Well, that must be a different Charles.'

'Are you telling me that I don't know my own brother?'

Charles can see that the old man is obviously mad.

'No, no, of course not,' Charles says hurriedly, and tries not to have any more conversation with him.

◆

Dinner is served, and everybody begins to eat. Laura, the bride, is very happy, and laughs and talks with everyone near her. Even Angus is smiling, which is unusual for him. In England it is a custom for the best man to make a speech and at last it's time for Charles to stand up. He hits a glass loudly with a spoon, and people stop eating and talking. Charles is nervous.

'Ladies and gentlemen, I'm sorry to take you away from your conversation and the wonderful food, but there are a few things that I need to say. This is only the second time that I have ever been a best man. I hope that I did the job well the first time. Well, the bride and groom are still talking to me! Unfortunately though, they're not talking to each other.

'But people say that I'm not guilty. Yes, I did say in my speech that Piers, the groom, had slept with Paula's younger sister. But Paula knew this already – she really did! She was a bit surprised to hear that he had also slept with her mother. But I don't think their violent two-day marriage broke up because of that. I really don't think so!'

Most people burst out laughing at the joke – Carrie is one of them – and some clap, but there are a few straight faces.

'But of course I'm here today to talk about Angus, and he has nothing to hide, has he? Well, that's what I thought at first . . .'

People are still laughing, as Charles becomes serious for a moment.

'I'd like to say that I do think very highly of people who get married, like Angus and Laura. Marriage is a big step to take, and I know I couldn't do it. But I think it's wonderful that they can. Now, back to Angus and those sheep!'

Everybody laughs and claps, and then Charles asks them to raise their glasses and drink to Angus and Laura.

♦

After the formal dinner and speeches, it's time to dance. The band plays, and Laura and Angus as bride and groom are the first to come out on to the dance floor. Laura enjoys herself, and dances in a very lively manner, but Angus moves stiffly. Perhaps he's never heard pop music before. Scarlett and Tom dance together. They are both enthusiastic dancers; Scarlett dances wildly, and Tom very badly, but they enjoy themselves enormously. Gareth is dancing like a madman.

'When I first saw Gareth dance,' Matthew tells Charles, 'I thought to myself, "People will be killed. Lives will be lost." '

But Charles is not really concentrating on what Matthew is saying. He is looking for Carrie. When he sees her, she is already dancing with another man.

'She's pretty, isn't she?' Matthew notices that Charles is looking at her. 'Is it love?'

This may be true, but Charles is surprised and alarmed to hear Matthew say it.

'Oh, good God no – no, it's the man that she's dancing with! I was at school with him. I'm just trying to remember his name! But – well, if one did meet somebody nice at a wedding – are there men who could ask a girl to go out with them at once? On the same day, I mean?'

'If there are,' said Matthew, 'they're not English.'

'Exactly!' said Charles. 'I mean – it usually takes me about three weeks to ask.'

By about nine o'clock, it's getting dark, and the bride and groom are almost ready to leave. Laura has drunk a lot by now, and she is enthusiastically kissing some of her distant cousins, who she doesn't really know.

'They promised me sex,' says Lydia. 'Everybody said it. "If you're a bridesmaid, you'll get sex," they said. 'But has it happened? No, it hasn't. Nobody has been near me.'

'You know that I love you, Jean, don't you?' she asks, almost in tears. She puts her arms around Jean. 'I love you, I love you and Mike very much. I've never met you before, but I love you both, I really do.'

'Don't worry,' says Angus, her new husband. 'She's drunk. Well, I hope she is – or I'm in real trouble!'

Back in the tent, Lydia, the young woman who was a bridesmaid at the marriage service, is sitting with her head in her hands. She looks depressed. She is still wearing her bridesmaid's dress and the flowers around her head.

'How's it going, Lyds?' asks Bernard.

'Awful. Just awful,' complains Lydia.

'Oh dear. What's the problem?'

'They promised me sex,' says Lydia. 'Everybody said it. "If you're a bridesmaid, you'll get sex," they said. "All the men will want you. You'll have to fight them off." But has it happened? No, it hasn't. Nobody has been near me.'

'Well, look . . .' said Bernard, a little shy now, 'I mean – if you like – I could –'

'Don't be stupid, Bernard. I'm not desperate!' answers Lydia sharply.

'No, no, of course not – sorry – I just thought –' Bernard replies hurriedly.

◆

When the bride and groom are finally ready to get in their car, Laura throws her bunch of flowers at the guests. The person who catches it will be the next person to get married – or so people believe. Scarlett raises her hand to catch it, but fails. Fiona steps out of the way. And Lydia is the one who catches it!

The car has a string of tins tied to it, and rude things written on it. This is the custom at English weddings. But when Angus and Laura open the door, a large white sheep jumps out, with a bell tied around its neck! Everybody laughs. They all wave and shout goodbye as the happy couple are being driven away. They are going on their honeymoon.

Charles is sad, though, as he goes back into the tent. The band is playing 'Love is All Around'. Obviously, he feels that it's not true for him. Later on, his group of friends begin to make their arrangements for the night.

'Where are you staying tonight, Charles?' asks Tom.

'Scarlett and I are going to some pub – The Lucky Boat? Something like that. Aren't we all staying there?'

'Well, no – the plan has changed. The others are all coming back to my place. Nansy's there – you know, our lovely old servant. She'll probably cook us some bacon and eggs when we get there, and we could play some games. Would you like to come too?'

'Yes, excellent, thanks very much. Is there a room for Scarlett, too?'

'Oh of course – we've got a hundred and thirty-seven rooms actually.'

Tom's 'place' is his family castle. The house in London is not their only home.

'Tom,' asks Charles, 'are you the richest man in England?'

'Oh – no, no! I believe we're number seven on the list. Well, the Queen comes first, obviously. And that Richard Branson man is doing very well with his pop music and his aeroplanes.* Well, excellent news – I'm glad that you're coming. I'll go and tell Scarlett.'

Suddenly Carrie appears next to Charles.

'Hi!' says Charles, surprised. 'I thought you'd gone.'

'No – not yet. I was just wondering – where are you staying tonight?'

'Well, I was going to stay at some pub – The Lucky Boat?'

'Boatman,' Carrie tells him. 'The Lucky Boatman.'

'Right. But now I'm going to stay with some friends at their house. Well, I say house, but it's really an enormous castle . . .'

'Oh, what a shame – because I'm staying at the Boatman.'

'Oh!' says Charles, surprised again. This is really a perfect invitation – but he doesn't reply quickly enough. He is, unfortunately, an Englishman!

'Well – it was nice to meet you. Though we didn't quite meet,' says Carrie. 'I liked your speech – it was great.'

'Thanks,' says Charles. He still finds it hard to say anything, and they stand there silently together for a moment.

'I'm going now,' Carrie says.

* Richard Branson, a British businessman, owns the famous Virgin company.

'No – don't! Couldn't we meet each other now? The evening's just starting!'

They both look around at the tent, which is now in quite a mess, with bottles and chairs lying on the ground.

'We both know that's a big lie,' says Carrie, and she walks away.

'Hell!' says Charles.

The band has stopped playing, but the bride's sister and boyfriend are back with their guitar. Only four people are trying to dance now to their music, which is not very lively. Others are kissing, and a few really drunk people have fallen asleep. One of the pairs that are kissing is Bernard and Lydia. They are kissing very enthusiastically, and Lydia is quite breathless.

'Bernard!' she cries in surprise. 'I didn't know that it could be like this!'

'God,' says Gareth, looking around at all the mess. He hates the music that is being played. 'What a disaster! It's time for the castle. How about you, Tom – are you drunk? Can you drive us safely?'

'Of course, of course,' says Tom. 'I've had nothing to drink the whole evening.' But when he stands up, he nearly falls over! He must have drunk more than he thinks!

◆

The group of friends get into Tom's big car, and they drive away through the quiet countryside under the stars. They're trying to sing, but they're finding the high bits quite difficult.

Charles says, 'Tom, can you stop the car?'

Tom brakes suddenly.

'Sorry,' Charles apologises. 'I think I *will* go to the pub.'

'But why?' asks Tom.

'Ah –' Charles is uncomfortable, and doesn't know exactly what to say.

Everyone makes a joke of it.

'No, seriously,' says Charles. 'I'm writing about pubs that have the word "boat" in their name. My book will be the first on the subject.'

'Do what you like,' says Tom, and Charles jumps out. He is now standing in the dark in the middle of a road, somewhere in the countryside. He suddenly feels very much alone. And how is he going to find this pub?

'Hmm, an odd decision,' says Charles to himself.

He sets off in the opposite direction down the dark country road. He does manage to find his way to the pub, though by the time he arrives, it is about one o'clock in the morning. It seems very quiet in the hotel reception where Charles should check in. Charles is just about to ring the bell on the front desk when he sees Carrie. She is sitting peacefully in a large, comfortable chair.

'Hello,' says Charles.

She looks at him with a question in her eyes, but she is smiling too.

'Hi.'

'There wasn't enough room for everybody,' Charles lies, 'so . . .'

'You said it was a castle,' Carrie reminds him.

'Did I? Yes, that's true – it *is* a castle. But it's a very small one. Only one room upstairs and one room downstairs – very rare!'

They both enjoy the joke.

A waiter comes in and asks Charles, 'Would you like a drink, sir?'

Charles orders a drink for himself, and one for Carrie too. But when he turns round, there *is* no Carrie – where has she gone? Then George walks down the stairs. He is the boring man who read loudly in church. He is whistling and he seems happy. Charles understands.

'You're here too!' says George.

'Hello,' says Charles.

'You haven't seen Carrie, have you?' George is still speaking loudly.

17

'Who?' asks Charles, thinking fast.

'Carrie. American girl. Lovely legs. Wedding guest. Nice smell.'

'No – sorry,' answers Charles.

'Damn. I thought I had a good chance with her!'

Suddenly, Carrie's head appears above the sofa, where she has been hiding. She makes a terrible face to show that he had no chance with her at all! Only Charles can see, fortunately.

'Look, if you see her, could you tell her that I'm in my room?' asks George, not very pleased.

'Yes, yes,' says Charles, hoping that he'll go away quickly.

But just then, the waiter comes back with the two drinks.

'One for you, sir,' he says, 'and one for the –'

'One for the road!' says Charles brightly, before the waiter can say 'lady'.

'Actually, I think I'd like a drink too! Can I join you?'

'Yes – lovely idea,' says Charles unhappily.

'Another drink here and a cigar!' George calls out to the waiter. 'No, let's have a bottle! We'll drink till daylight, eh, Charles?'

Charles sits down on the sofa, and George on a chair. Charles knows Carrie is behind the sofa. She is trying to escape.

'Lovely wedding,' says George.

'Yes,' says Charles, wondering how he can get away.

'I was at school with Angus's brother, Buffy. Excellent man, though he liked little boys too much. Still, it taught me a few of life's lessons. Where do you know the bride and groom from?'

'Angus and Laura? Oh, from university,' answers Charles. He is not exactly enjoying the conversation.

'Yes, yes, excellent place. I didn't go to university myself though. I work in the money markets, you know. What good are books there? Not much at all.'

'Excuse me sir.' The waiter is back again. He has a message for Charles. 'Your wife asks you to go upstairs at once. Room Twelve. She said that you may be too drunk to remember the number.'

'My wife?' asks Charles, in surprise.

'Yes, sir,' the waiter replies.

'Oh – yes, of course, my *wife*!' Charles says, as he understands.

'You must be drunk!' says George. 'You can't even remember whether you've got a wife!'

'Yes – will you excuse me?'

'Oh yes, off you go! Good luck! Well, I haven't got a wife, so I'll go and look for that Katie woman.'

'Carrie,' says Charles.

'Yes, that's the one. A fine girl. I think I might be lucky there!'

◆

Upstairs, Charles knocks on the door of number twelve. He is quite nervous. Carrie opens it.

'Hi,' she says.

'Hello. I'm sorry about that.'

'No, that's fine – it was impossible to get rid of him.'

'Yes – perhaps we should just wander about up here for a bit, then go back down.'

'That's a thought,' says Carrie. 'I don't usually wander, but I *can* wander if I need to. Do you wander a lot?' She is gently joking with him.

'No,' says Charles, still nervous, 'I'm not really a wanderer – I don't usually wander a lot but –'

'Well,' Carrie says, 'why don't you come in and wander here a little, and then we'll see?'

She leads him into the room.

'It's strange,' she says. 'The bride and bridegroom didn't kiss in the church. Where I come from, kissing is very popular.'

'Is it? Yes, I think you're right.' Charles is speaking fast. 'I think English people are probably more shy.'

'I always worry,' continues Carrie, 'that I would go too far in the church – you know, at the place in the marriage service

19

Carrie kisses Charles on the mouth.

where the groom can kiss the bride. I might not stop at kissing –'

'How far is too far?' asks Charles, coming very close to her.

'Oh, I don't know.' She gives him a very small kiss on the cheek. 'That would be all right, I think.'

'Yes,' says Charles. 'That would be fine.'

'Perhaps it's not enough,' says Carrie. 'Maybe this would be better.' She kisses him on the mouth.

'Yes. But it might be dangerous to go further,' says Charles, nervous again.

Then they kiss for a long time.

'That might be too far . . .' says Charles.

'And this?' asks Carrie. It is a few minutes later, and they are in bed, making love. 'Do you think the priest might be a little bit worried about this?'

'Yes,' says Charles. 'I think he might be.'

They kiss again, and spend the night together.

◆

The pub is in the middle of the countryside. It looks very peaceful in the morning. Carrie gets up first and packs. When Charles wakes up, she is already zipping up her bag. Her face looks beautiful in the early morning light.

'What's happening?' asks Charles.

'I have to go,' she answers.

'But where to?'

'To America.'

'That's a tragedy,' he says.

'But before I go, when are you going to tell everybody?' Carrie asks him.

'Tell everybody?' Charles asks in surprise. 'Tell them what?'

'Well, you'll tell them that we're going to get married, won't you?'

'Get married?' He is alarmed now.

'We slept together last night – we made love – so that means we're getting married, doesn't it?'

'Well – yes – oh dear – we need to think hard about this, you know,' he says unhappily.

Then suddenly he notices she's smiling.

'Oh, you're joking!' he says. 'Thank God! For a moment, I thought I was in one of those awful films. You know – the kind where the woman spends a night with a man and murders him if he won't marry her.'

'No,' says Carrie, gently. 'We're not in one of those films. But I think we've both missed a great chance here. Goodbye!'

She leaves the room and Charles lies down in the bed. He looks thoughtful and confused.

Chapter 2   The Second Wedding

*You are invited to the wedding of Bernard and Lydia at noon on
August 1st at the Church of St Mary of the Fields,
Cripplegate, London EC2*

It is three months later, and Charles's alarm clock is once again
ringing by his bed. Charles stretches out his hand and turns it off. He
goes back to sleep again. He likes to sleep until noon, whenever he
can. Scarlett is still asleep in her untidy bedroom. Some time later,
there is a loud shout from Charles's room. He has woken up, at last.

'Oh hell!'

He jumps out of bed, and runs in to Scarlett, dressed only in
his underclothes.

'Oh God!' says Scarlett, when she looks at her clock.

They run out of the house before they have finished putting
on their formal wedding clothes. Scarlett is trying to put on a
silly pink dress with an enormous skirt, but she can't zip it up
right. She is going to be a bridesmaid.

'Car or taxi?' she asks, still running.

'Taxi,' says Charles. 'We won't be able to park the car.'

They get to the corner of the street and start looking for a
taxi. But there isn't one anywhere.

'Well, maybe the car is a better idea,' says Charles.

They rush down another street to find Scarlett's car. But when
they get there, it can't be moved. Scarlett must have parked it in
the wrong place and the wheels have been locked by the police.

'Damn!' they both shout at once.

They will have to go on foot. They run as fast as they can.

'The service will start before we get there,' Charles thinks to
himself.

Charles and Scarlett get to the corner of the street and start looking for a taxi. But there isn't one anywhere.

The skirts of Scarlett's silly pink dress fly up in the wind and, as she runs, a piece of the dress falls off.

Charles is going to stop and pick it up, but Scarlett says, 'Leave it! Nobody will notice!'

They run all the way to the church, and as they get near, they can hear the bells ringing loudly. Some of their friends are already there – Fiona, Matthew, Gareth and David.

'Sorry I'm late,' says Charles. 'The traffic was awful.'

They all look at him; nobody believes him at all.

'Yes, well –' says Charles. 'Now, who's getting married today?'

He reads the wedding card, pretending that he doesn't know.

◆

They all go into the church, where the wedding is about to start. A young priest comes in, looking worried and nervous. It's Father Gerald, who they met at the last wedding reception. He's finished his studying, and now he's a real priest.

Today Tom is best man. He has remembered to bring the rings, one each for the bride and groom. He takes them out of his pocket and shows them to Charles, holding them up to his eyes like a pair of glasses. Charles smiles and waves at him.

As the wedding music starts, the bride and her bridesmaids enter the church. The bride, of course, is Lydia, who first kissed her bridegroom, Bernard, at the last wedding reception. There are four bridesmaids. Two are little girls and two are women. One of them is Scarlett. As she walks up the aisle, everyone can see her bright blue underclothes. The piece of her dress that fell off has left a large hole in the back of her dress! Scarlett is still wearing her sunglasses too – she looks quite strange! She takes them off just as they reach the priest. Bernard is standing there by the priest, waiting for his bride.

Father Gerald begins to read the words of the marriage service. Unfortunately, because he is very nervous, he gets some of the words wrong. Everybody bursts out laughing.

'It's his first wedding, you see,' Matthew whispers to Charles. 'He's a friend of the family.'

'Ah. Excellent,' says Charles. He finds it very amusing.

Father Gerald calls Bernard 'Lydia' by mistake. And when he does get the groom's name right, he doesn't know how to say Bernard's middle name. It's written 'St John' and spoken as 'Sinjun'.

'. . . Bernard Geoffrey Sijjjjjjjern Delaney,' says Father Gerald, hurriedly. Everyone is smiling. This is all very entertaining.

Now, as the priest speaks, the bride and groom have to repeat the same words after him.

'I Bernard Delaney –' says Father Gerald, leaving out the St John part now. 'Do take you, Lydia Jane Hibbott, to be my awful wedded wife.' This is not what he should say at all! He is so nervous that he's getting the words mixed up!

'To be my *lawful* wedded wife,' Bernard says. These are the words Father Gerald should have said.

'That's right. That's right,' says Father Gerald. He doesn't know exactly what he's doing now, but somehow they get to the end of the service.

'Well done!' shouts Gareth, clapping, and the others copy him. It's like being at the theatre, and after the service, everybody congratulates the priest. Gerald is very pleased with himself, and is smiling too, now that it's all over.

◆

The reception is being held in an elegant London hotel. The guests seem to be from rich, upper-class families. All the men are wearing formal wedding coats, and the women are in expensive dresses. Lydia, the bride, is in an excellent mood; she is laughing and kissing the guests as they arrive. Charles, Gareth and Matthew have already found the drinks. They are used to weddings, and know exactly what to do.

'Do you know what I think about marriage?' asks Gareth. 'Two people are in love. They live together, then suddenly they can't think of anything to say to each other. They're worried – what are they going to do? Then the man has an idea.'

'What?' asks Charles.

'They'll get married! And then they've got something to talk about for the rest of their lives.'

'So – people get married when they can't communicate properly any more. Is that what you're saying?'

'Yes, that's right. Tom!' Tom, the best man, has come to join them. 'How's the speech?'

'Fine – good, I think. Something for everyone – yes, the jokes will raise a few smiles, and there should be a few tears too,' Tom says.

'Excellent!' says Gareth.

'It's an interesting idea, Gareth,' says Charles.

'Of course, there's another idea. Some people think that weddings are about true love,' says Matthew, looking at Gareth.

'Well, that's a thought,' Charles replies lightly. But he has listened seriously; Charles is very confused about love and marriage at the moment.

The reception is very busy now, full of well-dressed guests who are drinking and chatting, laughing and calling to one another.

Charles is just fetching three more drinks, when a voice says, 'Hi.'

He turns round. It's Carrie. She looks wonderful.

'Hello,' says Charles, and nearly drops the drinks.

'How are you?' asks Carrie.

'Fine. Fine. Sorry – I'm so surprised, and so pleased to see you. Don't go back to America! Please! Wait here – I'll be back in two seconds. OK?'

'OK,' she smiles.

He rushes back to the others.

'That's yours. And that's yours,' he says, giving them their drinks. 'See you in five hours.'

'Has something happened?' asks Gareth.

'Yes – yes – this is a great wedding, you know!'

But when he finds Carrie again, things don't quite go as he planned.

'Hi. You look perfect. In fact, you probably *are* perfect. How are you?'

'I'm really well. Charles, I'd like you to meet Hamish. Hamish and I are going to get married.'

This is a horrible shock for Charles, but he tries to hide it.

'Excellent, excellent. I'm happy to meet you, Hamish. Lovely surprise to find Carrie back in this country again.'

Hamish is an elegant and confident man of about fifty. He is Scottish.

'Yes, well, it wasn't easy! I had to work hard – she didn't want to come at first. Come on, Carrie dear, I want you to meet James. He's waiting for us over there. He'll think that I can't control you at all, if we don't go and find him now!' He holds out his hand to Carrie, and she takes it.

'I'll see you later,' she says in a friendly way to Charles, as she walks away with Hamish.

Charles is shocked and very unhappy. He is unhappy about Carrie, of course, but why is he so *very* unhappy? He doesn't quite understand himself at the moment. He doesn't feel in the mood to join in with the party any more, and he sits down alone. Later, Matthew comes up to talk to him.

'How are you doing, Charles?' Matthew asks.

'Actually, not great,' says Charles. 'Not great at all, really. I don't know – what's happening here? Why am I always at weddings but never getting married? What does it mean?'

'You're not smart enough,' says Matthew. 'Or perhaps it could be because you haven't met the right girl.'

'Ah, but is that right?' Charles asks. 'Maybe I have met the right girl. Maybe I meet the right girls all the time. Maybe it's me – I'm the problem.'

'Oh, rubbish!' says Matthew.

♦

And then it's time for dinner. Everyone has been told to look at a written table plan to find out where they have to sit. It has all been organized very carefully.

'Come on,' says Matthew, 'you'll probably meet your future wife at dinner.'

Charles looks at the table plan. 'Oh my God!' he says, but doesn't tell Matthew why he is so alarmed.

♦

Fiona is already sitting at another table, next to an upper-class older woman who is wearing a bright blue dress and a bright blue hat. Her name is Mrs Beaumont.

'Are you married?' she asks Fiona immediately.

'No.' Fiona answers.

'Do you prefer women?' asks Mrs Beaumont.

'Good God!' says Fiona. 'What made you say that?'

'Well, it's a possibility these days, isn't it?' Mrs Beaumont says. 'And it's an interesting one. It's very boring if you just say, "Oh, dear, I've never found the right man!"'

Fiona laughs. 'Quite right. Why be boring?'

'Thank you,' says Mrs Beaumont.

'Well,' Fiona continues, 'I have met the right person, you see. But he's not in love with me. Until I stop loving him, I can't get interested in other men.'

'Bad luck,' says her new friend.

'Yes, isn't it?' says Fiona. 'I did go with another girl once, at school – but it was only for about fifteen minutes. I don't think that really means anything, do you?'

♦

Charles has now found his table, and sits down with two men and four young women, who are all attractive and about the same age as him. His brother David is there too. Charles looks very embarrassed and uncomfortable.

'Hi,' says Charles to one of the men.

'Hello, I'm Alistair. You know Veronica, don't you?'

'Yes,' says Charles, very nervous now. 'Yes – hello Vee! Hi, Nicki! Great to see you.' He can see Carrie on another table. She's laughing with Matthew and Gareth. Charles would much rather be at their table.

Alistair seems to be giving them all a lesson on tea. 'There are about four hundred different kinds of tea, and all the fruit teas as well. I took Veronica out to India at Christmas to see the places where they grow it.'

'Excellent,' says Charles.

'You and Veronica went to India together, didn't you Charles?' Alistair asks.

'That's right,' Charles answers. So Veronica was once a girlfriend of Charles's.

'Charles was horrible,' says Veronica. 'I was really ill, and he just joked all the time.'

'I was only trying to make you feel better, Vee.'

'Oh, you're *that* Veronica,' says Nicki.

'Which Veronica?' Veronica asks. 'Charlie – what have you been saying?' She's worried too now.

But Charles doesn't want to answer the question. 'Remember Bombay?' he asks brightly.

Nicki continues. 'When Charles and I were going out together,' – so she's another old girlfriend of his – 'he told me about this "interesting" journey he'd taken round India with "Vomiting Veronica". Yes, I think that's right. I'm sure that's what he called her.'

'Did I really say that?' asks Charles quickly. 'No I don't think so –'

'Oh come on, Charles,' says Martha, who is old girlfriend number three at the table. 'You could never keep a secret. You're hopeless.'

Charles is certainly in a horrible mess now.

'Martha, that's not quite true –'

'I'm sure it is, Charles,' says Nicki.

'I remember another thing you told me,' Martha continues. 'About a girlfriend that you had called Helena. Her mother liked you too. She wanted to go to bed with you! You told me that you didn't know what to do. "Would it be rude to refuse her?" you asked yourself.'

'That's right!' adds Nicki. 'You said that they were both as fat

29

as pigs! Mrs Piggy, and Miss Piggy –'

'I think perhaps –' says Charles, but the three girls are laughing loudly and they're not listening to him.

Finally, the fourth girl, who is sitting quietly next to him, speaks. 'We've both lost weight since then, my mother and I,' she says, taking another chocolate.

It is a disaster for Charles. But fortunately it's now time for the speeches.

'Ah – great – speeches!' he says. At least they can't talk about him any more until later.

Everyone claps Tom as he stands up.

'Yes – when Bernard told me he was getting married to Lydia, I congratulated him. All his other girlfriends were real dogs, you see! And of course, I'm delighted to see so many of them here this evening . . .'

It is a terrible speech, but Tom thinks he is doing well. So does Gareth! He seems to enjoy really awful things.

'Camilla is one of them – it's lovely to see you again, Camilla! She was the first person who Bernard wanted to marry. She told him to go to hell! It's lucky for Lydia that she did!'

When the dinner and the formal parts of the reception are over, Charles and his friends are free to meet up again. They find some comfortable sofas, and sit down together to chat.

Gareth is talking about the wedding dinner. For once, he is not being rude. 'We had a lovely girl at our table – Carrie. She's going to marry a man called Hamish. He's very rich and owns half of Scotland. So, how are you?' he asks Charles.

'This is the wedding from hell!' Charles answers. 'Old girlfriends everywhere. I'll probably meet Henrietta next. That'll really finish the day off for me!'

'Hello, Charles,' a voice says from behind him. It's Henrietta and, of course, she's also one of Charles's old girlfriends. Charles seems to have no luck at all today. Henrietta is a tall, dark girl, and she is usually quite attractive. But now her face is white, and she looks very unhappy. Charles is feeling bad, but Henrietta seems to feel even worse.

'Hello, Hen, how are you?' says Charles brightly, trying to pretend that everything is all right. He hopes that she did not hear his last few words.

She is silent for a moment, then she bursts into tears.

'Oh, Hen,' says Charles, sympathetically.

Helena jumps up from the sofa in a temper. 'Why can't you just leave her alone? Haven't you hurt her enough?'

She leads Henrietta away.

Charles gets up. 'Excuse me,' he says to Gareth. 'I think I am a walking disaster at the moment. I think I'd better go away and be alone.'

◆

But not everyone is having a bad time. David, Charles's brother, is talking to Serena, the pretty girl who was interested in him at the last wedding reception. She has been hoping to meet him again, and has started to learn sign language so that she can communicate with him.

She signs her name. 'I'm S-e-r-e-n-a.'

David smiles sweetly at her.

'Hello,' he signs back.

'I'm just learning,' says Serena with her hands. 'I'm probably making lots of mistakes.' She certainly is – she signs 'tols' instead of 'lots', and 'nistakes', instead of mistakes. But David doesn't want to correct her. He shakes his head and smiles again.

'No, perfect. Perfect,' he tells her. 'Would you like to dance?'

'Yes, that would be nice,' Serena replies. They go off together, looking very happy.

◆

Charles is in a bedroom upstairs. It seems to be empty – the door was open, but there was nobody inside, just a suit hanging up on a cupboard door. It's dark now, but he doesn't turn the light on. He goes to the window and looks down on to the street below. He just stands there quietly, glad to be alone in a calm room. But after a minute or two, he sees Carrie down there. She's coming out of the hotel with Hamish. They have their arms around each other and look very happy. They get into a taxi together. Charles watches them unhappily as they drive off. He seems to be very depressed.

Then the door opens, and Bernard and Lydia come in, kissing noisily. They are so interested in each other that they don't notice Charles. They are still dressed for the wedding – Lydia in her bride's dress, and Bernard in his suit. This is their room, the place where they are going to change into their other clothes before they go away on their honeymoon.

But they're not ready to change yet. They are about to have sex on the bed. Charles wonders how he can escape, and he begins to try to walk from the window to the door very, very quietly.

Then suddenly Lydia cries, 'Wait a minute! This isn't good enough! I want to see my lovely husband!'

She turns on the light. She is lying on top of Bernard – she still has her dress on, but Charles knows what's happening underneath it. Luckily, they don't see Charles. But he can't get past them to the door. Then he sees another door nearer to him, so he opens it and goes through it as fast as he can. Oh, no! It's only a kind of very small washroom – no more than a cupboard, really! There's almost no room in it for Charles! He waits there; it's very uncomfortable, and it seems to him that he has to wait for hours.

♦

Downstairs, the other guests are enjoying themselves. Several of them are dancing to the lively music. Scarlett is sitting in a strange place, like Charles upstairs. She's under a table with one of the small bridesmaids. They are both dancing to the music but only using their hands for the dancing movements.

'Have you got a boyfriend?' Scarlett asks the little girl, whose name is Freda.

'Yes,' says Freda.

'What's his name?'

'Dolph. He's good at table-tennis. And you?'

'No. No boyfriend.'

'Why not?'

'I don't know,' says Scarlett, a little unhappily. 'When I like men, they don't seem to like me. They think I'm stupid. Then, the ones who like me – well, I think *they're* stupid! I don't want to go out with them. So that doesn't get me anywhere, does it?'

♦

Upstairs, in the bedroom, time passes. Lydia and Bernard are still making love, very noisily. Charles is sitting on the basin in the washroom. He looks at his watch.

'God, are they going to finish soon?' he wonders. If he'd known they were going to take so long, he wouldn't have hidden there.

'Oh – I love my wife!' cries Bernard.

'I-love-my-husband!' screams Lydia.

They finish. After a quiet moment or two Bernard says, 'We'd better go downstairs now, I suppose.'

Charles nods. 'Yes! Yes!' he says silently to himself.

'Or,' says Lydia, 'we could wait a few minutes – and start again!'

'No, no!' Charles shakes his head inside the cupboard.

He really can't stay there any longer, so he opens the door. He walks past Lydia and Bernard who are still lying on the bed. They are amazed and stare at him in great surprise, but he pretends that

33

it's not strange at all. He holds up a pencil as he walks towards the door of the room.

'I found it!' he says, and goes out.

♦

But his troubles are not over. Henrietta is outside.

'Charles, we must talk,' she says firmly.

'Right, right,' he says pleasantly. Is this a bad dream? But he would rather talk to Henrietta than stay in the bedroom with Bernard and Lydia!

They start walking downstairs together.

'The thing is, Charlie, I've spoken to lots of people about you.'

'Oh, God!' says Charles.

'And everyone agrees that you're in real trouble, Charles,' she continues seriously.

'Am I?' he asks.

'You see, you have one girlfriend after another, but you don't love any of them. You never let a woman get close to you at all.'

'No, no, Hen, it's not like that −' says Charles.

But it's no good. Henrietta continues, 'You're nice to them, sweet to them − you were sweet to me, though you thought I was stupid.'

'I didn't.'

'Yes you did. You don't give people a chance. Whenever you have a new girlfriend, you think, "I mustn't fall in love. I mustn't get married." '

'Hen, you know me! I don't think like that! Most of the time − well, I don't think at all!'

'Oh, Charlie!' Henrietta suddenly throws her arms around him. 'The way you used to look at me! I thought − I thought that you were going to ask me to marry you! But you were only thinking about how to leave me. Oh − this is awful!'

She walks away. She is very upset. Charles just stands there. He can't move. Actually, he doesn't know what to do. Then he turns round and sees Carrie behind him.

'Are you having a good time?' she asks him.

'Oh, yes, of course! Wonderful – better than my father's funeral! Really entertaining!' Charles says. 'I thought you'd gone.'

'No – Hamish is going on the night train to Edinburgh. I just went with him to the station. But I *am* leaving now. Do you want to come with me?'

So Charles and Carrie drive off together through the late-night streets of London. The taxi takes them to Carrie's flat.

'Are you coming up for a drink?' she asks Charles.

'Are you sure?' he asks. He looks rather doubtful about the situation.

'Yes – I think we can take a chance!' she jokes. 'You're attractive – but I can still refuse you, no problem! You're not *so* attractive, you know!'

Charles is not feeling very confident after all the horrible things that have happened today, so he doesn't share the joke. 'OK. Yes. Great.' he says, without a smile.

But as soon as they are together in Carrie's flat, it's like the last time that they met. They kiss, and become lovers again. They are both very happy to be with each other, and they spend the night together. But Carrie is still going to marry Hamish. Charles has left it all too late.

In the early morning, Charles gets up first. He puts on his formal wedding suit again; he doesn't have any other clothes with him. He looks at Carrie for a long moment, and she looks back at him. She is very beautiful. They seem to be in love and Charles doesn't want to go. Finally, he turns and leaves the room quietly. What would have happened to the couple if Charles hadn't been so confused?

Chapter 3   A Free Saturday

It is nearly noon on Saturday, September the 1st. Charles is in bed, asleep as usual. The door opens, and Scarlett comes in, carrying cups and plates and the morning letters.

'Good morning, Charles. I've brought us some breakfast. Sorry the toast's a bit burnt.'

She sits down on the edge of the bed. Charles wakes up. Scarlett pours the tea and spreads butter on the toast. They eat breakfast together comfortably.

'What are you going to do today?' she asks him.

'Well,' says Charles, 'today is a day without a wedding. A free Saturday!* The only thing that I have to do is to meet David. I mustn't be late for him.' He picks up a large white envelope and opens it.

'I think I'll look for a job today,' says Scarlett. 'I heard about one the other day, as a shop assistant. You have to sell strange clothes to strange people. I think I'd be good at it.'

But Charles isn't concentrating. He is studying the card in the envelope. He looks rather upset.

'Are you all right?' Scarlett asks him.

'It's that girl, Carrie – do you remember? The American girl. It's the invitation to her wedding.'

♦

The invitation also tells guests the address of the shop where they can buy presents for the bride and groom. This is another custom for some people in England. It seems that Charles is still going to spend his time today on weddings.

---

* In Britain, most weddings happen on a Saturday.

*But Charles isn't concentrating. He is studying the card in the envelope.
'It's that girl, Carrie – do you remember? The American girl. It's the
invitation to her wedding.'*

The shop is horribly expensive. There are handmade carpets,
there is furniture from different parts of the world, and the place
is full of all kinds of unusual and beautiful things.

The shop assistant is also very elegant. She looks down her
nose at Charles, who is wearing an old shirt with his shorts and
running shoes. He doesn't look at all smart.

'Excuse me,' he asks her. 'Do you have the wedding list for
Banks? Hamish and Carrie Banks?' Carrie Banks is what Carrie
will be called after her marriage to Hamish.

The assistant looks at Charles with dislike. 'Certainly, sir. I can
show you plenty of presents for about one thousand pounds.'

'Ah!' says Charles, who is amazed, but is trying not to show it.
'What about presents for fifty pounds?'

'You can buy this one,' says the assistant. She points to a life-
size wooden African man.

'This?' says Charles. 'Excellent!'

'You can buy it,' the assistant says nastily, 'if you can find someone to pay the other three thousand, nine hundred and fifty pounds.'

Charles smiles. He is still being very polite and trying to look calm.

'Or we sell plastic bags for one pound fifty pence each,' she continues. 'Why don't you just buy thirty-three of them?'

'Actually, I think I'll probably leave it. Thanks very much. You've been very...' He was going to say 'helpful', but it wouldn't be true.

As he turns round to go out of the shop, Carrie walks in.

'What did you get?' she asks him, smiling. She looks very happy.

'Oh – nothing, nothing yet! I've just been looking,' says Charles. It is once again a surprise to meet her. He is always delighted to see her, but he never knows what to say.

'It's nice to see you,' she says.

'It's nice to see *you*,' says Charles.

'It's great, getting presents,' says Carrie. She laughs. 'Why didn't I get married years ago? Has anybody bought the wooden African yet?' she asks the assistant.

'The young man is thinking about it,' says the assistant, icily polite.

Charles nods thoughtfully, trying to look as if this is a serious idea.

'Oh no,' says Carrie, who is quick to understand. 'Get me something small – a teapot or something. Are you free for about half an hour?'

'Yes – I have to meet my brother, but – I can be a little bit late.' It's a lie. David will be annoyed if Charles is late. But he doesn't want to miss the chance to spend some time with Carrie.

'Good,' she says. 'Come with me. I've got to make an important decision.'

◆

She takes Charles off to the dress shop where she plans to choose her wedding dress.

'The most important thing', she says, 'is – please don't laugh!'

'OK. Right,' says Charles, seriously.

The assistant brings dress after dress. Carrie takes each one away and tries it on. Each time, when she's ready, she comes out and shows Charles. The first dress is very complicated, with full skirts.

'What do you think?' she asks him.

'Lovely!' says Charles.

'Isn't it a bit like a cake?' she asks him.

'Well –' says Charles.

'Don't worry,' says Carrie. 'I thought so too! But we've only just begun.'

She comes out next in a very modern style of dress. Actually, it is not really a dress at all – it's a suit with trousers, a long open coat, and a very small top. Sexy!

'What do you think this time?' asks Carrie.

'You're joking!' says Charles.

'But it's wonderful, isn't it? Maybe next time . . .'

The next dress is long, in a 'country girl' style, like an old eighteenth-century picture. It is quite sweet, but not right for Carrie.

'What do you think?' she asks again.

'Ah –' says Charles.

'I knew it!' she says, smiling, and goes behind the curtain to take it off.

Then she comes out in a very simple, but very sexy dress.

'It's a bit sexy,' she says.

'If I was your husband, I'd be so proud,' says Charles, and he means it. 'But maybe you're right. You don't want the priest to get too excited!'

After Carrie has chosen her dress, they go to a café together to drink tea. It has started to rain now.

'Marriage is strange,' says Charles. 'Just one man and one woman – no more lovers, ever! Do you think you'll stay faithful?'

'Yes, once I'm married,' Carrie replies. 'I told Hamish that I would kill him if he goes with another woman. So I'd better do the same, I think, and leave other men alone.'

'Quite right,' says Charles.

'And I've had plenty of lovers in my life,' she continues.

'Have you?' asks Charles, surprised. 'How many is "plenty"?'

'Well – oh I don't know,' says Carrie, a little bit embarrassed. 'More than one.'

'Tell me!' says Charles. 'There are no secrets between us now. I've seen the wedding dress, remember?'

'Well –' says Carrie, and she starts to count on her fingers. 'The first one, of course, you never forget. It was nice. Number two – he had too much hair on his back! Three – four – five – number six was on my birthday, in my parents' bedroom.'

'Which birthday?' asks Charles quickly.

'My seventeenth,' she answers.

'Seventeen? You got to number six by your seventeenth birthday?'

'I grew up in the country – it's different there,' she says. 'OK – seven was good. Eight – rather small! That was a shock! Nine – we were standing up against a gate. Never try it, Charles. It's very uncomfortable.'

'I won't,' he promises her seriously.

'Ten was wonderful, really like heaven.'

'I hate him,' says Charles.

'Eleven – no good. Numbers twelve to seventeen were during my university years. They were all nice, intelligent boys – but the sex wasn't much good. Eighteen broke my heart. I couldn't forget him for years afterwards.'

'I'm sorry,' Charles says.

'I don't remember number nineteen. But my girlfriend says that it did happen – twice. She shared my room, so she should know. Twenty – are we really at twenty? God! Twenty-one – horrible! I don't want to talk about him. Twenty-two – well, he was always falling asleep! That was my first year in England.'

'I must apologize for England, and Englishmen,' says Charles.

'Twenty-three and twenty-four were together – I won't forget that!'

'Seriously?' asks Charles, but she won't answer him. He is not sure how much of this is serious at all.

'Twenty-five was a lovely Frenchman. Twenty-six was an awful Frenchman. Twenty-seven was a mistake.'

'Suddenly, at number twenty-seven, you made a mistake?' asks Charles. 'Can this really be true?'

'He kept on screaming,' says Carrie simply. 'I nearly gave up sex after that. But Spencer changed my mind for me. He was number twenty-eight. Then there was his father, number twenty-nine.'

'Spencer's father?' Charles repeats.

'Then thirty – horrible! Thirty-one – oh my God! Thirty-two –' she pauses. 'Thirty-two was lovely. And then there's Hamish, number thirty-three.'

'So I was – after Hamish?' asks Charles. He really wants to know now.

'No, you were thirty-two,' replies Carrie, and Charles thinks about this.

'That's it, then,' says Carrie. 'Less than Madonna, more than Princess Diana – I hope. What about you? How many people have you slept with?'

'Not as many as you!' Charles answers. 'I probably don't have enough time. What do I do with my time? Actually, I don't really know. I work – yes, that's it! Work, work and more work. I'm always working late!'

Carrie and Charles both stop talking. There is a very serious, silent moment; something has happened, and they both feel it.

Carrie laughs. And suddenly, they both stop talking. There is a very serious, silent moment; something has happened, and they both feel it.

'I wish I'd phoned you,' says Charles. 'But you didn't ring me.' Then he looks at his watch. 'Oh, hell! Help me, please! I'm late – again!'

♦

When they reach the cinema, David is still waiting outside. If it hadn't been his brother he would have probably left by now. Charles is very, very late. David signs to him, 'You're not my brother any more! You're just some stupid fool that I once met!'

'Carrie, this is David, my brother,' says Charles. 'This is Carrie,' he signs.

42

'Hi,' says Carrie.

'We were buying a wedding dress for her,' Charles signs.

'That's a really poor excuse,' David replies. 'Who's she marrying?'

They can now have a secret conversation, because Carrie doesn't understand sign language.

'A real fool,' says Charles.

'How does a fool find a beautiful wife like her?' asks David.

Carrie is waiting for a translation.

'Yes, I'm just telling David that you're marrying Hamish. "What a lucky man!" he said to me.'

'Didn't you make love to her once?' asks David. Fortunately, Carrie still can't understand.

'He wants to know where you are getting married,' Charles pretends to translate.

'In Scotland,' Carrie answers.

'She's got lovely breasts!' says David, and uses his hands to describe them.

'"Oh, lovely hills up there in Scotland," he says!' Charles translates quickly.

'Why don't you come to the wedding?' Carrie asks David. 'I'd like some nice friends to come – Hamish is going to invite some awful people. Well, you'd better go in and see the film. Goodbye!'

The brothers watch her as she walks away. Charles and David go into the cinema, but suddenly Charles changes his mind.

'Oh, hell!' he says.

He runs out of the cinema and chases Carrie up the steps. David is left alone at the entrance to the cinema. Charles catches up with Carrie by the river.

'Carrie! – Sorry, sorry! Oh – this is stupid – you've just bought your wedding dress. But I wondered if there was any chance – no, obviously not! I've only slept with nine women – so why am I asking silly questions? But I just wondered – I really

43

feel – well, let me say it more clearly, like the man in the song. Or was it the man on television? "I think I love you." Would you perhaps like to – no, no, of course not! I'm a fool, and he isn't. Excellent. Excellent. Lovely to see you. Must go now.'

He turns to leave, then adds, 'Damn!'

'That was very sweet,' says Carrie. She is smiling at him and looks very affectionate.

'Well, I thought about it a lot, you know. I wanted to get it just right. It's important that I've said it.'

'What have you said, exactly?' asks Carrie.

'I said that I think – oh, you know what I said!' Charles is finding this very difficult.

'You're lovely,' says Carrie, and kisses him. For a minute, they stand close together, then Carrie walks away. She looks back at him one last time.

Chapter 4   The Third Wedding

You are invited to the wedding of Hamish and Carrie
on September 28th, in the church at Glenthrist Castle,
Perthshire, Scotland

It is already a cold, wet autumn in Scotland by the time of Hamish and Carrie's wedding. The mountains and lakes look very beautiful but also very gloomy and grey. Charles arrives late – as usual – and tries to change quickly out of the warm, heavy clothes that he put on for the journey. He takes off his pullover and puts on his wedding coat before he steps out of the car. The wedding is in the little church that belongs to Hamish's castle.

The door of the church makes a loud noise as Charles opens it. 'Sorry, sorry,' he whispers. Everybody turns round to see who's there.

The little church looks charming. The service has begun, and Carrie is standing with Hamish and the priest at the front. She looks lovely, too – serious, but beautiful. The priest asks Hamish whether he will take Carrie for his wife.

'I do,' says Hamish.

He asks Carrie whether she is willing to take Hamish for her husband.

'I do,' answers Carrie.

'Damn, damn, damn it to hell!' whispers Charles as violently as he dares. His last hope has disappeared.

◆

The reception is in the fine castle that Hamish owns. As the guests walk there from the church they can hear special Scottish music being played. When they arrive, they are welcomed by

45

servants who are wearing formal Scottish uniforms. Among the guests, many of the men are wearing Scottish-style clothes too and some of the ladies are also dressed in the Scottish style. The bride, the groom and the family are standing in a line. The guests shake hands with them as they come in. Carrie is standing at the end of the line, next to Hamish. Charles congratulates Carrie.

'You look beautiful,' he says as he shakes her hand.

There is some lively Scottish dancing in the middle of the room.

'Oh, great!' says Gareth. 'It's like one of those films! It's so Scottish that it can't possibly be true!'

He joins in the dancing enthusiastically.

'Dear friends,' he says a little later, when his usual group of friends is standing together at the edge of the room. 'None of us is married. You know, I was always proud of that. Not a wedding ring between us! But now, I'm getting older, and it's suddenly begun to make me sad. I'd like to go to the wedding of someone who I really love.'

'Well, don't blame me!' says Tom. 'I've asked everybody that I know to marry me!'

'You haven't asked me,' says Scarlett, a little sadly.

'Haven't I?' asks Tom in surprise.

'No,' she shakes her head.

'Well, Scarlett – would you like to marry me?'

'No thank you, Tom. It was very nice of you to ask me.'

'Well, any time you like,' says Tom kindly.

'Good man, Tom!' shouts Gareth. 'Now, why don't the rest of you do the same? Go and find husbands and wives for yourselves! Those are your orders for tonight. But first we'll all drink to "True Love!"'

'What about you, Fi?' Tom asks his sister. 'Can you see a husband here?'

'Oh, get lost, Tom!' replies Fiona.

'True love!' They all raise their glasses.

Tom takes the idea seriously. He tries to talk to a pretty woman, 'A lot of people actually meet their husbands and wives at weddings. Did you know that?'

'Yes, I met my husband at a wedding,' she answers him.

'Oh. Oh well,' says Tom, and drinks the rest of his wine very quickly. 'Look at that! My glass is empty. Excuse me –'

Scarlett seems to be having better luck. The person she is talking to is probably the best-looking man at the wedding. And he's not wearing Scottish clothes – he's American.

'Hello, my name's Scarlett. Like Scarlett O'Hara in *Gone with the Wind*,★ but I'm much less trouble than she was! What's your name?'

'My name's Rhett,' says the American.

'No – from the same story? Not really?'

'No, not really,' he smiles. 'My name's Chester.'

'You're a joker!' Scarlett laughs. 'When I meet Americans, I always think that they're going to be boring. But of course, you're not boring, are you? You're lovely!'

Scarlett has to look up a long way when she talks to Chester. He is very tall and she is short. It looks quite funny.

Charles is hiding from Henrietta, but she soon finds him.

'Oh, hi, Hen! Sorry – I didn't come to talk to you because I really don't want an argument today. I'm sure that we've got lots to talk about, but not today, Hen, not today!'

'Did I behave badly, last time?' Henrietta asks.

'It was quite frightening,' says Charles. 'Like a murder film.'

Henrietta laughs – she is in a good mood. Charles decides that he's safe with her today, and so he goes on talking to her.

'Oh, Hen, I'm depressed,' says Charles. 'What about you? How are you?'

★ A famous film and novel. Scarlett and Rhett are the names of the two most important people in it.

47

'Well, I'm quite happy actually,' she says. 'I've got a new boyfriend and my weight's down to almost nothing.'

'Perhaps you were right, Hen,' says Charles. 'Perhaps we should have got married.'

'God, no!' says Henrietta. 'I don't want to marry your friends too, specially Fiona.'

'Fiona loves you,' says Charles.

'Fiona calls me Duck-Face,' says Henrietta.

'I've never heard that!' says Charles.

Henrietta knows that he's lying. 'Come to lunch sometime,' she says. 'Give me a ring.' She gives him a gentle kiss on the cheek.

As she walks away, Fiona comes up to Charles. 'How's Duck-Face?' she asks.

'She's fine, actually,' says Charles. 'Not too mad at the moment.'

♦

'Ladies and gentleman,' says the best man. 'The bride and groom!'

Hamish and Carrie dance together in the middle of the room. It's a formal Scottish dance and everybody claps them. Charles and Fiona watch the happy couple with the other guests. Fiona puts her hand on Charles's shoulder and looks at him. She can see that he looks sad.

'You like this girl, don't you Charles?' asks Fiona.

'Yes — it's a strange thing, this love business, when at last it happens . . . and now she's marrying another man,' answers Charles. 'But what about you, Fifi? Have you met your future husband here?'

'No — and I won't — it's not like that. I've been in love with the same man for years.'

'Have you?' Charles asks in surprise. 'Who's that?'

'You, Charlie,' says Fiona, very lightly. Charles stops smiling. He looks shocked. Fiona walks away and goes into a quieter room. Charles follows her.

'It was always you, ever since we first met,' says Fiona. 'I knew that from the first moment I saw you. "Across a crowded room" – you know what they say! But it doesn't matter. We can't do anything about it. That's life. And we're friends – "friends" isn't bad, you know. It's quite good, really.'

Charles is upset, and he feels her pain. A few months ago, he didn't know love, but now he knows how it feels. He is deeply sorry for her, and takes her hand.

'Oh, Fi! It's not easy, is it?'

'No. But forget it – it can't happen between us, Charlie.'

Just then, Matthew comes in. Fiona pretends that nothing has happened.

'Matthew dear!' she says brightly. 'Where's Gareth?'

'He's being rude to Americans,' Matthew answers.

'How thoughtful of him!'

Gareth is dancing with an American woman. She looks surprised as he turns her round fast and jumps about quite

Gareth is dancing with an American woman.

49

violently. Tom is dancing too, and looking hopefully at every girl in the room. He clearly hasn't found his future wife yet!

When it's time for the speeches, Gareth comes back over to his friends, very hot.

'Ladies and gentlemen, fill your glasses, please,' says the best man. 'Unusually, the bride will make the first speech.'

'Excellent,' says Gareth. 'I love this girl!'

He looks at Charles – he knows about Charles's feelings for Carrie now.

'Thank you,' says Carrie, as everybody claps her. 'And thank you to those people who've flown in from the United States. Congratulations to the rest of you! You came here, even though you knew that all these terrible Americans were coming too!'

People laugh, and Charles looks at Carrie with love.

'My dear Dad should be the one to give this speech. But, sadly, he's not alive today. If he was here, I know what he would say: "Lovely dress, girl! But why the hell are you marrying a man in a skirt?" '

They laugh again, though Hamish is not very pleased with this joke about Scottish clothes.

'My answer is,' Carrie continues, ' "Because I love him." As John Lennon said, "Love is the answer." And we all know that.'

The guests clap loudly. Charles can't believe that he has been so stupid. Why did he let her go? If he hadn't been so slow he would have been the groom here today.

'Oh, one more thing!' says Carrie. 'Someone here said that if things didn't go well with Hamish, he would be ready to take his place. Well, thank you, and I'll let you know!'

It is a very cheeky thing to say, but Hamish laughs loudly. He begins to make his speech now, very confidently. Hamish is not self-conscious. He has had years of practice in public speaking. Suddenly there is a loud noise, a kind of crash, at the back.

'Oh dear – someone doesn't agree with me!' he jokes. 'No problem! I'm used to that!'

But the crash was Gareth, falling unconscious to the floor. Charles, David and Tom get to him quickly.

'Find a doctor,' says Charles, urgently. While Hamish is still speaking, a doctor is found among the wedding guests. He gives Gareth a quick examination. Then they carry him into a quieter room, and put him down gently on the ground. Charles is on his knees, holding Gareth's head. But it's too late. Gareth is dead. Then he decides that he must find Matthew quickly among the crowd of guests.

Charles sees Matthew and walks towards him. Just before he reaches him, he stops – it's a hard moment. Then he moves forward, takes Matthew's arm and whispers to him. As he tells him about Gareth they can hear the guests behind them begin to sing.

Chapter 5   A Funeral

It is the day of Gareth's funeral. It takes place in the town where Gareth's parents live, a small and dirty town, full of factories. Gareth didn't come from a rich family. It is raining and grey, and everyone looks very sad. It is a big contrast to the three wonderful weddings. Matthew and Gareth's family are driven to the church in a large black car. In front of them is the car with Gareth's coffin.

Charles arrives at the church and sits down next to Fiona, putting his arm around her. Carrie is there too, quiet and white-faced at the back. The atmosphere is very different from the atmosphere at the weddings. Everybody is wearing dark clothes and nobody is talking.

'Good morning,' the priest welcomes everybody. 'Welcome to you all, on this cold day. Our service will begin in a few minutes, but first we've asked Gareth's closest friend, Matthew, to say a few words.'

Matthew steps forward and stands near the coffin. It has beautiful flowers on it.

'Gareth preferred funerals to weddings. "One day I shall probably have a funeral," he said, "but a wedding – never!"'

People smile and begin to feel a little bit more comfortable.

'I rang a few people and asked them about Gareth. What did they think about him? What comes into their minds when they hear his name? Well, a lot of people said, "Fat." And a lot more said "Terribly rude." So "very fat and very rude" was the way that strangers described Gareth. But then some of you here rang me and said that you loved him. You remember visiting Gareth, and how kind he was to his guests. You remember what an adventurous cook he was. Fortunately, the secrets of some of his

Matthew steps forward and stands near the coffin.

dishes, like duck with banana, are lost for ever! Gareth really loved life. I hope you will remember him specially for that.

'How do I remember him? I can't find the words – I'm sorry. So I've taken the words of another writer. This is what I really want to say.'

He reads from a book:

> *He was the stars and the moon in my sky,*
> *the most joyful hello and the sweetest goodbye.*
> *Every day, every moment, our love was my light,*
> *and now I'm alone in the dark of the night.*

After the service, people meet and talk outside. It was a very emotional funeral and everybody looks very sad. The car with

Gareth's coffin is driven away.

Charles finds Carrie. 'It's good of you to come,' he says. 'But didn't it spoil your honeymoon?'

'Oh, it doesn't matter,' says Carrie. 'We'll do it another time. You know, that thing you said in the street . . .'

'Yes, I'm sorry about that,' Charles says quickly.

'No, don't be sorry. I liked it. I'm glad that you said it.' She kisses him gently on the cheek, then walks away. He watches her go.

'Would you like a walk, Charlie?' asks Tom.

'Yes – good idea.'

'I've never felt like that,' says Tom. 'Not like Matthew. Not that kind of love. Well, I felt something for Jilly when I was young –'

'Jilly?' asks Charles, surprised.

'Our family dog,' Tom explains.

'Yes . . .' says Charles. 'It's strange, isn't it, we've all been friends for years, and we never noticed that Matthew and Gareth were really married, in their own way.'

They have reached the river, but it is not an attractive place – there are factories all along the banks. Everything looks cold and gloomy. Charles is holding an umbrella as it is still raining.

'It's hardest for his parents,' says Tom. 'I hope I die before my children.'

'You're very confident that you'll get married,' says Charles. 'But should we get married at all, if we can't find the right person? We saw today at the service that there *can* be a perfect marriage. And if we can't be like Gareth and Matthew, perhaps we should just forget the idea. Some of us won't get married at all.'

'I don't know, Charlie,' says Tom, thoughtfully. 'I don't hope for the perfect marriage. I'm not looking for thunder and lightning. I just want a nice, friendly girl who likes me too. Then we'll get married and be happy. It worked for my parents – well, it did for years, until they separated . . .'

'Then I give you six months at the most, Tom,' replies Charles. 'You won't have to wait any longer than that. It'll happen before then, you'll see. And maybe you're right. Maybe waiting for true love is quite useless.'

Chapter 6   The Fourth Wedding

You are invited to the wedding of Charles and — on July 15th
at St Julian's Church, Smithfield, London EC1

It's Charles's wedding day, but even now he's not awake! His male friends gave him a special party last night, and everybody drank too much! The alarm clock rings, Charles turns it off. He gets ready to go back to sleep again. But then another bell rings, and another!

'What the hell's happening?' he asks. He looks around the room. There are twenty or thirty alarm clocks in there with him!

Tom has been sleeping next to him. 'I decided that we mustn't be late!' he says brightly. 'I like your hair-style – excellent for a wedding!' Charles's hair is a total mess. He gets out of bed and goes into the kitchen, still in his underwear. Matthew is already there; he's going to be Charles's best man. Unlike Charles, he looks very smart.

'Matthew – great!' says Charles, sleepily. 'Listen – thanks for doing this today! I wish Gareth was here.' He knows what a hard time Matthew has had recently.

'He'd like to be here too,' says Matthew. 'Sorry we're so late. The others are just parking the car. We thought that we could all go in Tom's car because it's so big.'

'Late? Is it so late?' asks Charles.

'Yes – it's 9.45.'

'Nine forty-five?' Charles can't believe it.

'Only forty-five minutes until you say, "I do." '

'Oh God! I wanted the alarm to ring at eight o'clock! I *told* Tom! Oh, hell!'

Now Scarlett comes in, still in her nightdress. Her hair looks terrible too and she is yawning.

'Scarlett?' Matthew says. 'Are you ready?'

'Oh yes, yes –' she answers sleepily. 'Just give me twenty seconds!' And she makes herself a cup of coffee.

They drive as fast as they can to the church. Charles is still putting on his tie when he gets out of the car.

'What's the time?' he asks urgently.

'Honestly?' asks Matthew. 'You really want to know?'

'Yes – *tell* me, please!'

'Well,' says Matthew, 'it's about ten to nine.'

Charles keeps on running towards the church, then suddenly he realizes what Matthew said.

'You rats!' he shouts. His friends all start laughing; they changed the time on all those clocks. If they hadn't played this joke Charles would have been late for his own wedding!

♦

They've got plenty of time now, so they get some coffee and drink it outside on the grass. Fiona decides to make a speech.

'I'll just say a little word,' she begins. 'I've watched Charles's girlfriends come and go for years now. I was worried that he would never get married! But now everything's going to be fine. Unfortunately, his bride is quite crazy – but perhaps that's why he loves her! So let's drink to Charles and his beautiful girl on this sad day. Be happy – and don't forget us!'

'Thank you,' says Charles.

'To Charles – and Duck-Face!'

They raise their plastic coffee cups and drink.

'Thank you, Fiona, for those few kind words about my future wife!' Charles replies. 'She's sent a message for you, too!' He pulls out a piece of paper and reads – or pretends to read – from it. ' "If any of you come near my house, I'll send the dogs out to get you!" '

Charles pulls out a piece of paper and reads – or pretends to read – from it. ' "If any of you come near my house, I'll send the dogs out to get you!" '

Everyone laughs, and they set off for the church. Today, perhaps for the first time ever, Charles won't be late!

♦

John is one of the first guests to arrive. He's the man whose wife was still seeing Toby de Lisle. And he's actually Henrietta's brother.

'Hope my sister arrives,' he says to Charles. 'You can't have a wedding without a bride, you know. And why didn't you have a party last night?'

'Oh, but we did, we did – we didn't think it was a good idea!' says Charles hurriedly. John, of course, was not invited to the party!

'You look lovely today, Fi,' Charles says to Fiona, as they enter the church together. She's wearing a smart jacket of red, blue and other colours.

'Yes,' she replies. 'I decided that I wouldn't wear black any more.' Usually, Fiona chooses black or dark colours for her clothes. 'From now on, I'm going to wear bright colours, and find somebody who'll fall in love with me. That'll be different, won't it?'

'You're a dear girl,' says Charles, and gives her a friendly kiss.

Charles stays alone in the church. He walks around and looks rather uncomfortable and nervous. He doesn't look as happy as bridegrooms usually look on their wedding day.

Outside the church, Scarlett and Matthew are welcoming the guests. As usual, Scarlett is wearing something strange – this time it's a formal wedding suit, but made in a man's style. It looks quite sweet on her, but a little bit odd. Suddenly, she screams! Chester has come – her tall, charming American from Carrie and Hamish's wedding. She is delighted!

'I thought that you'd gone back to America!' she says, excitedly.

'Without you?' he asks. 'Never!' And he gives her a big kiss.

An old man appears at the door. It's the crazy man who sat next to Charles at the first wedding!

'Bride or groom?' Matthew asks him, so that he can show him where to sit.

The old man looks at him angrily. 'I'm neither!' he says. 'Can't you see?'

Tom is looking after a young lady called Deirdre.

'Bride or groom?' he asks her.

'Bride,' she says. She looks like a nice girl – very gentle and pretty. But for Tom, it's something more. It's love at first sight!

'Haven't we met before?' he asks her.

'Yes, we have, about twenty-five years ago. We're cousins – well, distant cousins!' she smiles at him. 'You're Tom, aren't you?'

'So you're family! Wonderful — well, do sit here, Deirdre,' he says.

'Good God!' he tells himself, as he walks away. 'Thunder and lightning!'

Charles is even more nervous now, as he sees all the guests coming in.

'Good luck!' says the priest, passing by.

Lydia and Bernard arrive together, and Charles goes over to welcome them.

'How are you?' he asks.

'Very tired, actually,' says Bernard.

Then Charles suddenly sees Carrie, who has come alone. He didn't have any idea that she was coming. She's looking elegant but she seems to be in a quiet mood, and a little sad.

'Hi!' he says. 'You look lovely. But then you always look nice at weddings!'

She smiles at him.

'How's Hamish?' he asks.

'Oh, he's fine — I think,' she says.

'You think?' asks Charles, surprised. 'What do you mean?'

'He wasn't the right man for me after all,' she says.

'You've left him?'

'We left each other,' she tells him. She looks quite weak, and Charles leads her to a quiet place at the side of the church where they can talk.

'When did this happen?' he asks her.

'Oh, a few months ago. March was hell. But by April, we'd made all the decisions and it was OK. I won't marry someone so old again!' She tries to turn it into a joke, but obviously she is not very happy.

'Charlie!' calls Matthew. 'Time to go!'

'Yes, yes — I'm coming,' says Charles, not really listening to him. 'But why didn't you ring me up?'

'Well, I thought about it,' Carrie replies, 'and I wanted to — but things were so difficult then. You'd better go now. I'll see you later.'

'I'll show you to your seat,' Charles says. 'We just didn't get it right, did we? If only we'd been together at the right time . . .'

'Yes, we got it wrong,' Carrie says sadly.

'Terrible. Awful,' says Charles, and he means it. 'But it's so lovely to see you!'

'Well, good luck,' says Carrie finally. 'It's very easy, you know, getting married. You just say, "I do" whenever anyone asks you a question.'

'We'd better go to the front,' Matthew tells Charles.

'Can you give me a moment, Matthew?' Charles asks him.

'Of course,' says Matthew, who thinks that Charles wants to go to the toilet.

◆

But Charles is no longer in the right mood for his wedding. He goes into an empty side room and says, 'Dear God, please forgive me for what I am going to say in your church – Damn! Damn! Damn and hell!'

'Can I help you?' asks a sympathetic voice. A priest steps out from behind a curtain in the same room, where he was washing his hands. It seems that the room was not empty.

'Oh – no, thanks!' says Charles, embarrassed. 'I was doing some exercises – you know, for my voice. This is a big church!'

'Excellent, I often do the same myself – I use rather different words, of course. I'll leave you alone now.'

Charles still cannot come back out into the church, and Tom and Matthew are getting worried.

'The bride's arriving now,' says Matthew. A large black car has driven up to the church and Henrietta gets out with her father. She is dressed finely for the wedding, in white, with flowers in her hair.

'Well, that's great,' says Tom. 'Because we've lost the groom.'

'Try to keep her outside for a bit,' says Matthew. 'I'll go and look for Charles.'

'Matthew!' says Charles brightly when he sees his best man. He is very unhappy. 'Good to see you! Tell me – what do you think about marriage?'

'Well –' says Matthew, uncertain how to answer this. 'I think that it's really good, if you love the other person with all your heart.'

'Exactly,' says Charles. 'But I've been to so many weddings, and now it's my own wedding day – and I'm still thinking.'

'What are you thinking about? Can I ask?'

'No, no – better not,' says Charles.

Tom is now standing at the church door, talking to Henrietta and her father. 'I'm terribly sorry,' he says. 'The service will be a few minutes late. There's a problem with the flowers.'

'With the flowers?' asks Henrietta. 'What problem?' She clearly doesn't want any problems on her well-planned wedding day. Henrietta gets annoyed very easily.

'Well,' says Tom, thinking hard, 'they are making some people ill, so we have to move them.'

Henrietta and her father look angry, but they wait at the door. People in the church are getting restless now too. They're wondering what's happening. The bride must have arrived by now. Where is the groom?

'I think they believed me!' Tom tells Scarlett. He is pleased with himself. 'People think I'm stupid, you see. So they don't realize that I can tell a clever lie!'

David has now joined Matthew and Charles in the side room. Charles still won't go back into the church. He is too unhappy and confused. David hits the table to make a noise, so that Charles will notice him.

'What's happening? Tell me!' he signs.

'Oh, God,' Charles signs back. 'I just saw Carrie. She and Hamish have separated.'

'Charles, it's your wedding day,' David tells him.

'What's your advice?' Charles asks.

'Well, you can do one of three things. Number one: just get married, as you've planned.'

Charles nods.

'Number two: you can go back and say, "Sorry – no wedding today!"' David continues.

'I don't like that idea,' says Charles. 'What's number three?'

'Number three –' signs David. 'Well, I can't think what that is.'

'Hell,' says Charles.

There is a knock on the door, and the priest comes in.

'Hello,' he says, smiling. 'Are you ready to meet the enemy?'

'Are we?' asks Matthew. It's not really a joke at all. Everyone looks at Charles.

'Yes,' says Charles. 'Excellent.'

◆

He tries not to look at Carrie as he walks to the front of the church and sits down. The wedding music starts, and Charles and Matthew stand up together. The doors at the back open, and Henrietta, proud and beautiful, walks down the aisle with her father.

She pulls at her father's arm. She is annoyed with him. 'Don't hold me so tightly, Dad,' she whispers angrily.

The priest begins to read aloud the words of the wedding service. As Charles listens to the priest's words he looks confused and worried. The priest asks whether anyone thinks that Charles and Henrietta should not get married. The question is in the wedding service because that is the law. If either the bride or the groom is already married, for example, then someone may say that they are breaking the law. Usually, of course, no one answers the question. But this time there is a loud noise. David is knocking on his wooden church seat.

63

'I'm sorry – does someone want to speak?' the priest asks, very surprised.

David puts up his hand.

'Yes – what is it?'

David, of course, can't speak aloud, so he begins to sign to Charles.

'One second,' says Charles, as he signs back. 'What's going on?'

'I thought of idea number three,' David tells him.

'What?'

'Will you translate?'

'Translate what?'

'What's happening, Charles?' asks the priest.

'Charles – *what*?' asks his bride.

'He wants me to translate what he's saying,' says Charles.

'And what *is* he saying?' asks the priest.

'He says: "I suspect that the groom is having doubts. I suspect that he would like to delay the wedding. I suspect that the groom ..."'

'Really loves another woman,' signs David. Charles does not translate this. 'It's true, isn't it, Charles? Think about it, because it's for the rest of your life, Charles. It's final. So you must only marry the person who you love with all your heart. And – your trousers are undone!'

It is a kind of joke, but Charles looks down at the zip on his trousers. He is totally confused.

'What's he saying?' asks the priest.

'He suspects that the groom loves another woman,' answers Charles.

'And do you? Do you, Charles?'

Charles is silent for a moment. Everybody in the church looks shocked. They are all staring at Charles. Henrietta is staring at Charles too. She can't believe this is happening.

'I do,' he replies, in the words of the wedding service.

Suddenly, Henrietta screams. She throws down her flowers and hits Charles hard in the eye. He falls over, and she hits and kicks him again. She has really lost her temper this time! She is very, very angry, and maybe a little crazy too. Some people rush to the front of the church to help Charles. Other people try to stop Henrietta attacking him. The situation gets very confused. The wedding is certainly not going to happen today!

◆

Back in Charles's kitchen later that afternoon, everyone is still shocked. Outside it is pouring with rain and the thunder crashes in the sky.

'My God!' says Scarlett. For once, she doesn't really know what to say.

'Well,' says Tom, trying to be helpful. 'At least we won't forget this wedding! I mean, a lot of weddings are the same, aren't they? Afterwards, you can't remember them at all. But this one was really different!'

'Yes – it didn't have a wedding service,' says Matthew, in a dry voice.

Charles doesn't say anything. He has a black eye.

'Poor girl,' says Fiona. 'No, I really mean it – poor girl! OK, she's not my favourite person in the world. But you've done a terrible thing, Charles – I think it's quite unforgivable.'

Charles is shocked too. He can't quite believe that he did this. 'Poor Hen,' he says, 'I don't even want to think about it, it's so awful.'

'But if you weren't sure that you wanted to marry her on your wedding day, then it was probably the right decision, wasn't it?' Tom asks.

Usually, Fiona is rude about everything that Tom says. But now she simply says, 'You're right, Tom,' and touches his cheek lovingly.

'It's a lovely dress,' says Scarlett. 'I'm sure it'll be useful for parties!'

'I blame myself,' signs David.

'What did he say?' asks Matthew.

'He says that he blames himself,' Charles translates.

'No!' shouts everyone together. 'No, you mustn't do that, David!'

'Yes, they blame you too!' Charles unkindly tells his brother.

The doorbell rings, and everyone gets up.

'No,' says Charles. 'I'll answer it. If there's a problem, it's my problem.'

But it's Carrie at the door. It's pouring with rain, and she's very wet.

'Hello,' she says.

'Hi! God, you're wet!' says Charles. 'Come in!'

'No, no, I'm fine,' she replies. 'I'm so wet that I can't get any wetter. Do you know what I mean?' She smiles at him, but she's also very serious.

'OK – then I'll come out,' Charles says.

'No, please don't!' says Carrie. 'I just wanted to see if you were all right. I wanted to make sure that you weren't killing yourself or anything.'

But Charles steps out and joins her in the rain. They stand together on the pavement, and after a few seconds, he is completely wet too.

'It was wrong of me to come to the church this morning – I'm sorry. I can see that you're OK, so I'd better go now.'

'No – wait – I'm to blame, not you,' says Charles. 'I behaved really badly today. But I'm sure about one thing now – marriage is not right for me at all. And I learnt another thing. When I was standing there in the church, I realized for the first time that I totally, completely love one person, with all my heart. And that person wasn't my bride. It's the person who's here with me now, in the rain.'

'Is it still raining?' asks Carrie. 'I didn't notice.'

'In fact, I've loved you since the first minute I saw you. You're not suddenly going away again, are you?' he asks in alarm.

'No, I might be washed away by the rain, but I'm not going away again.'

'OK, OK, we'll go back in,' says Charles. 'But first, can I ask you one thing? Do you think – do you think that you could agree *not* to marry me? After we've got dry again, of course. And after we've spent lots of time together. Do you think that you could agree *not* to be married to me, for the rest of your life?'

Carrie looks at him, her eyes very serious now.

'Do you?' he asks her.

'I do,' she answers, in the words of the wedding service.

They kiss – and above, in the stormy skies of London, there is thunder and lightning for Charles too.

And how does the future go? Well, if we move forwards in time and take some more photos, we see something like this:

A picture of Henrietta at *her* wedding. She's forgotten all about Charles now; she's marrying a handsome soldier. He's wearing a uniform with a red jacket, and she's laughing as they leave the church.

And here's a picture of Charles's brother David, marrying Serena. They both look very sweet – a good couple!

What about Scarlett? Yes, here's a picture of her – she's getting married to Chester, her big American. She's wearing something different, as usual – a white cow-girl hat.

There's a picture of Tom and Deirdre too, taken at their wedding reception. They're outside Tom's enormous house. Tom's black dog is in the photo too, and Deirdre is wearing the 'country girl' wedding dress that Carrie refused to buy.

Here's one of Matthew, looking happy again. He's found a new boyfriend. He's younger than Gareth – about the same age as Matthew. They're at a party together. It's good that Matthew can leave all his old sadness behind.

And Fiona? Who's she with? Well, it seems to be Prince Charles! They're not exactly married yet, but she's out with him in public. He looks serious, as usual, but she's wearing an enormous pink hat and has got a big smile on her face.

Charles and Carrie are still not married. At least, there are no wedding photos, so they can't have got married. They must have kept their promise. But they do have a baby – a lovely little boy. In our photo, Charles is pointing at the camera and Carrie is smiling. We can see that they're very happy together, and that they're getting on fine without the sound of wedding bells!

ACTIVITIES

Chapter 1, pages 1–7

Before you read

1 Look at the Word List at the back of the book. Find words to complete this description.

On the wedding day, the church was full of flowers. The guests were all in smart clothes, and some looked very **(a)** ..... . The wedding was supposed to start at **(b)** ..... . The **(c)** ..... arrived with her father at the church at two minutes to twelve. She got out of her car and her two **(d)** ..... ran to join her. They could smell burning and they could see smoke coming from behind a gravestone. The **(e)** ..... and **(f)** ..... were smoking **(g)** ..... . The bride's father whistled to the **(h)** ..... . He jumped up, ran into the church and up the **(i)** ..... . The best man followed him but tripped at the church door. '**(j)** ..... !' he said. He had torn his **(k)** ..... trousers on a **(l)** ..... nail. He quickly walked up the aisle. All the guests and the priest were staring at him. He felt very **(m)** ..... because most of them were laughing.

2 Read the Introduction at the front of the book. Are these sentences right or wrong?

   a At the beginning of the story, Charles is late for his own wedding.

   b Henrietta thinks Charles will soon find the right woman.

   c Carrie is interested in Charles.

   d The story is sometimes funny and sometimes sad.

   e Richard Curtis found the film very easy to write.

3 What can go wrong at weddings? How many things can you think of?

While you read

4 Choose the best answers.

   a Who usually brings the bride's ring to the wedding ceremony?

      1) the priest   **2)** the groom   **3)** the best man

b Who or what wakes Charles on the morning of Angus's wedding?

    1) his alarm clock **2)** the sun **3)** Scarlett

c What's wrong with Charles's car?

    1) it won't start **2)** it won't go fast **3)** it's too old to drive

d Who drives backwards on the motorway?

    1) Charles **2)** the lorry driver **3)** Scarlett

e Whose ring does Charles give to the priest?

    1) Scarlett's **2)** Fiona's **3)** Gareth's

f What does Fiona think of Carrie?

    1) she's pretty **2)** she's quiet and shy

    3) Fiona doesn't like her

After you read

5 Answer the questions.

  a Why is Charles a bad choice for a best man?

  b How are Charles and Scarlett similar?

  c Why doesn't Charles tell Angus that he has forgotten the ring?

  d Why is Charles surprised by the ring that Matthew gives him?

  e Why does Gareth pretend to shoot himself?

Chapter 1, pages 7–14

Before you read

6 Charles is very interested in Carrie. This is the information he has about her: *Vogue*, America, black hat.

    What can he say to start a conversation with her?

While you read

7 Match the people with the descriptions. Write a–i.

a	the bride's father	..... sits down and kisses a stranger
b	John	..... a very proud man
c	Gerald	..... a crazy and dangerous dancer
d	Serena	..... not interested in Bernard
e	Scarlett	..... dull, with an unfaithful wife
f	the bridegroom	..... interested in Charles's brother

g Gareth ..... doesn't smile and can't dance
h Englishmen ..... embarrassed by Fiona
i Lydia ..... shy with women

After you read

8 Work in pairs. You are John and his wife after the wedding reception. You are driving home.

Student A: You are John. Ask your wife about Toby de Lisle.

Student B: You are John's wife. Pretend you don't know what he's talking about. Try to sound innocent.

Chapter 1, pages 14–21

Before you read

9 When the bride and groom leave for their honeymoon, it is a custom to tie tin cans to the back of the car. These bang along the road when they drive away. Describe a wedding custom in your country.

While you read

10 Choose the best words in *italics* to complete these sentences.

a *Fiona/Lydia* catches the bride's bunch of flowers.

b Tom's *London/country* house has a hundred and thirty-seven rooms.

c Charles decides to stay the night at the *castle/Lucky Boatman*.

d Carrie *goes upstairs/hides behind the sofa* when she sees George coming into the bar.

e *Carrie/Charles's wife* sends a message down to Charles.

f Carrie *wants to/doesn't want to* marry Charles.

After you read

11 These events take place at a traditional British wedding. Put them in the correct order 1–9.

a a photographer takes photos outside the church

b the best man gives the priest the ring

c everyone sits down to eat, and the best man makes a speech

d the bride and groom leave for their honeymoon

e the bride and groom's friends tie tin cans to their car

f the bride and her father arrive at the church

g the groom and guests arrive at the church

h the priest begins the service

i the wedding guests eat, drink and then dance

Chapter 2

Before you read

12 Look at the photograph of Charles and Scarlett on page 23. What's happening in this picture, do you think?

While you read

13 Draw lines to join the sentence halves.

a Charles and Scarlett	see Carrie at the wedding.
b Tom is the best man	future husband to Charles.
c Father Gerald makes	four old girlfriends.
d Charles is pleased to	are late again.
e Carrie introduces her	but he meets Henrietta.
f Charles has to sit with	Carrie invites him home.
g Charles is bored in	and Bernard's best friend.
h He gets out of the room	many mistakes.
i Charles is lucky because	Bernard and Lydia's room.

After you read

14 Why do these people get upset at the reception?

a Veronica

b Helena

c Bernard's old girlfriends

d Charles

e Scarlett

f Henrietta

15 Chapter 2 ends with a question: 'What would have happened to the couple if Charles hadn't been so confused?' What is the answer in your opinion?

Chapter 3

Before you read

16 Discuss these questions.

    a Fiona has said she is in love with someone who does not love her. Who is she in love with, do you think?

    b Why doesn't Charles ask Carrie not to marry Hamish?

    c Why did Carrie have sex with Charles although she is going to marry Hamish?

While you read

17 Are these sentences right (✓) or wrong (✗)?

    a Scarlett has a job.   .....

    b There are plenty of cheap presents on Carrie and Hamish's wedding list.   .....

    c The shop assistant is very polite to Charles.   .....

    d Carrie looks lovely in all the wedding dresses.   .....

    e Carrie says she has had thirty-three lovers.   .....

    f Charles was number thirty.   .....

    g Charles doesn't tell Carrie what David is really saying.   .....

    h Charles runs after Carrie and makes a very good speech about his love for her.   .....

After you read

18 Discuss this question.

    Carrie obviously likes Charles. There is something special between them. Why is she marrying Hamish?

Chapter 4

Before you read

19 Chapter 4 is called 'The Third Wedding'. Answer these questions.

    a Who is getting married this time?

    b Something unusual happens at this wedding. What do you think it will it be?

20 Who might say or think these words? Who to?

 a 'Why am I even going to this wedding?'

 .... to ....

 b 'I don't know your name, but would you like to marry me?'

 .... to ....

 c 'Which part of America are you from, and can I visit you there?'

 .... to ....

 d 'I know you can never love me like I love you.'

 .... to ....

 e 'My wife and I would like to thank you all so much for coming to our wedding.'

 .... to ....

 f 'I've got some terrible news. Gareth has had a heart attack.'

 .... to ....

After you read

21 How do these people feel at the end of Chapter 4, do you think?

 a Carrie

 b Hamish

 c Charles

 d Matthew

Chapter 5

Before you read

22 What usually happens at a funeral in your country? Talk about the time, the place, the people, what they wear and what they do.

While you read

23 Are the sentences true (✓) or not true (✗)?

 a Gareth's coffin arrives first at the church.   .....

 b Matthew arrives with Gareth's family in a black car.   .....

 c Everyone wears white.   .....

 d Matthew speaks to the people in the church.   .....

 e Matthew reads a poem that expresses his feelings about Gareth.   .....

f Carrie is annoyed with Charles for saying that he
loves her.   .....

After you read

24 Answer these questions.

   a What does Matthew's speech tell you about his relationship
      with Gareth?

   b What effect does their relationship have on Charles after the
      funeral?

   c What does Tom hope for in marriage?

   d Do you think Charles will wait until he finds true love?

Chapter 6

Before you read

25 Think about these questions.

   a Chapter 6 is called 'The Fourth Wedding'. Who will be getting
      married this time?

   b What do you think will happen to these characters at the end of
      the story?

   Charles   Carrie   David   Matthew   Tom   Scarlett

While you read

26 Who do these sentences describe? Write the names.

   a He thinks he is late for the wedding.   ....

   b She doesn't like Charles's friends.   ....

   c He wasn't invited to go out with Charles
      and his friends the night before the wedding.   ....

   d She comes to Charles's wedding in bright
      clothes instead of her usual black.   ....

   e She is very happy to see Chester.   ....

   f He falls in love with a distant cousin at the
      church door.   ....

   g She left her husband a few months before.   ....

   h She is annoyed because she has to wait
      at the church door.   ....

l He stops the wedding just in time. ....

j She goes crazy and hits Charles. ....

k He asks Carrie not to marry him. ....

After you read

27 Work in pairs. Fiona is left on her own at the end of the story. She has always loved Charles, but he has never loved her.

Student A:　You are Fiona. Tell your friend how you feel.

Student B:　You are Fiona's friend. Give your friend some advice.

28 There are a lot of funny moments in this story. Describe one that you enjoyed.

Writing

29 It is ten years later. How are Charles and Carrie? Describe what has happened in the last ten years.

30 Imagine Charles marries Henrietta after all. His brother doesn't stop the wedding. What will their marriage be like? Describe their lives one year later.

31 Imagine Charles and Carrie decide to get married after all. You are the best man at their wedding. You have to make a speech about Charles at the wedding reception. What will you say about him? Write your speech.

32 Carrie tells Hamish she is leaving. She packs her bags and takes the train from Scotland to London. Then she writes to Hamish. She explains her feelings and says how sorry she is. Write her letter.

33 The local newspaper hears about Charles's 'wedding' to Henrietta. A reporter interviews some guests and the priest at the wedding. Write the story for the newspaper.

34 After Charles goes off with Carrie in the rain, his friends back at the flat talk about them. Write their conversation.

35 Think of a celebration you have been to. Describe what happened: what were you celebrating, what did people wear, what did they say, what did they do? What special food and drink was there? Did you enjoy it?

36 'Without marriage, society falls apart.' Do you agree? Write arguments for and against marriage.

37 Charles is always late, especially for weddings. The film-makers almost chose 'Always Late' as the title of the film. Have you ever been late for anything important? What happened? Try describing the scene in the present tense, in the style of this book.

38 Imagine you work for a wedding planning company. One couple asks you to plan an unusual wedding for them: they want to get married in an unusual place, they want to wear unusual clothes and give their guests unusual food. Write a wedding plan for them, giving as much detail as you like.

WORD LIST

aisle (n) a long passage between rows of seats, in a church or plane, for example

best man (n) the man who helps the bridegroom (See below) on his wedding day

bride (n) a woman on her wedding day

bridegroom (n) a man on his wedding day

bridesmaid (n) a girl or woman, usually unmarried, who helps a bride on her wedding day

cigar (n) a thing like a cigarette but bigger and brown in colour

coffin (n) a long box in which a dead person is placed

cow-girl (n) a young woman who looks after cows and milks them

Damn! a word that some people use when they are annoyed; **damn** is also used like the word 'very' (not polite)

duck (n) a common water bird with short legs

elegant (adj) attractive and fine in appearance and movement

Father (n) the title for a priest in the Catholic Church

gloomy (adj) dark and sad-looking

groom (n) a man on his wedding day

honeymoon (n) a holiday for two people who have just got married

maid (n) a female servant, especially in a large house or hotel

nod (v) to move your head up and down to mean 'Yes'

noon (n) 12 o'clock in the daytime

rusty (n) covered in the reddish-brown substance that forms on old metal

self-conscious (n) worried about what you look like or what other people think of you

smart (adj) looking neat and suitable for a special occasion

undone (adj) not zipped, buttoned or tied shut.

vomit (v) to bring food or drink up from your stomach out through your mouth

wedded (adj) married

Better learning
comes from fun.

Pearson English **Readers**

There are plenty of Pearson English Readers to choose from –
world classics, film and television adaptations, short stories, thrillers,
modern-day crime and adventure, biographies, American classics,
non-fiction, plays ... and more to come.

For a complete list of all Pearson English Readers titles, please contact
your local Pearson Education office or visit the website.

pearsonenglishreaders.com